ROOKIE MISTAKE

MAREN MOORE

Copyright © 2024 by Maren Moore/R. Holmes
All rights reserved.
No part of this book may be reproduced in any form or by any electronic or mechanical means, including information storage and retrieval systems, without written permission from the authors, except for the use of brief quotations in a book review.

This is a work of fiction. Names, characters, places, businesses, companies, organizations, locales, events and incidents either are the product of the authors' imagination or used fictitiously. Any resemblances to actual persons, living or dead, is unintentional and co-incidental. The authors do not have any control over and do not assume any responsibility for authors' or third-party websites or their content.

Art: Jess Lynn Draws
Editing: One Love Editing

playlist

Passenger Princess- Nessa Barrett
Ain't No Rest For The Wicked- Cage The Elephant
Nothing's Gonna Hurt You baby- Cigarettes After Sex
"Goosebumps"- HVME
Again- Noah Cyrus
Obsessed- zandros, Limi
ANGEL- Toby Mai
Girls- The Kid LAROI
Teeth- 5 Seconds of Summer

Power Trip- J. Cole, Migos
Dangerously- Charlie Puth
"Into it"- Chase Atlantic

To listen to the full playlist click here!

For my girls who like it quick and filthy.
Davis Guidry is just the man for you.

chapter one
Zara

"Yeah" — Usher

"Oh my god, Zara, that guy up there is eye-fucking the shit out of you right now," my best friend Harper mumbles over the rim of her red Solo cup, her golden gaze trained on the dim, makeshift stage in front of us. "Biiiiitch, if you don't bid on him, *I* am."

It's not even midnight yet, and the house is already packed. Admittedly, the Kappa house is not my favorite place to party with the number of douchey frat guys and the stench of BO and stale beer, but there was no way in hell I was missing tonight.

Their annual *Date the Player* auction.

A night that even I, a new freshman at OU, have heard countless stories about.

I follow Harper's gaze out to the darkened stage in search of the guy she's referencing. There are no less than twenty up there, but I immediately spot him.

Holy shit… this guy *is* hot.

Like, *really*, really fucking hot.

And he's staring directly at me.

His pillowy lips are curved into a cocky grin, and when he catches my gaze, his thick, dark brow arches, something unspoken passing between us.

I lift a brow, mirroring the motion as my tongue darts out, wetting my lips and tasting the cinnamony remnants of the night's earlier Fireball shot.

Mystery guy's wearing a white long-sleeve that's rolled to his elbows, showing off thick, veiny forearms. The wrinkled fabric hangs open, unbuttoned, and even in the dim light, I can make out the washboard abs and a happy trail that peeks out.

He's got dark, unruly hair that kisses the top of his shoulders and what could possibly be the sharpest jawline I've quite literally ever seen.

As if his chiseled face was carved from the sharpest, most luxurious stone.

There's no doubt that this guy looks like trouble, and coincidentally, there is *nothing* I love more than trouble. Hmm.

Now, this could be *fun*.

Smirking, I lift my cup and bring it to my lips as I take a long, unhurried sip, never breaking our intense gaze.

"My god. I can *feel* the sexual tension from here. Or maybe I'm just horny. Either way... holy fucking shit," Harper nearly yells in my ear over the loud thrum of music surrounding us, her elbow digging into my side and forcing my attention back to her.

Her eyes are wide as she clutches her pink-painted fingers to her chest dramatically. They're nearly the same shade as the short minidress she chose for tonight. Unsurprisingly, she's decked out in all pink like she's the Gen Z version of Elle Woods.

Her signature color.

"You're the horniest person I know, so let's go with that, Harp," I tease, rolling my lips together before glancing to my right at Lily, the third of our thirsty trio.

Harper and Lily have been my best friends for as long as I can remember, and I've never been more thankful in my life that we all ended up at the same university because I don't know how I would have survived my freshman year without them.

A long-distance friendship with the girls who know

me better than anyone sounds like the worst form of torture.

We're codependent. They're my girls, and I need them by my side for what I already promised myself will be the best year of my life.

A year of being wild and free, without anyone or *anything* holding me back.

"You *both* are the horniest people I know, so that point is invalid," Lily says, shaking her head, causing the dainty pearl necklace around her neck to jostle with the motion. She's like the... mom of our trio.

The smart, responsible, dependable one.

Whereas I'm the wild child, and Harper is the party girl who somehow manages to keep straight As, even though she hasn't picked up a textbook all year and stumbles into class still slightly drunk from the night before on a regular basis.

Put us all three together, and we're perfectly balanced.

The loud, screeching sound of the mic slams through the speaker next to us, and the crowd groans with the sudden deafening noise.

"Yessss, it's finally starting!" Harper squeals, clapping her hands together excitedly. She reaches into the pristine white Gucci bag on her shoulder and pulls out the red auction paddles she picked up for each of us before the party started.

I wasn't planning on participating in the auction

Rookie Mistake

tonight, but after seeing mystery guy... I think I just might.

After all, it *is* for charity, and there's nothing I'd rather spend my father's money on than a good cause.

I see Lily begrudgingly pluck the auction paddle from Harper's grip, and I laugh before sliding my gaze back to the stage.

The crowd has nearly doubled in the minutes leading up to the auction, and the room is buzzing with electric anticipation. If it wasn't for the ridiculously large speaker we're standing near, then I doubt I'd even be able to hear the president of Kappa take the stage.

He taps a long finger on the top of the microphone. "This thing on? Hello, hello?"

"Yes! Now, bring out the guys," a girl screams from the staircase, giggling with her friends when the crowd cheers in response.

"Alright, I know y'all are excited and ready to get this going. I mean, tonight's a bit of an infamous night here at Kappa. We're going to have a fuckin' blast and raise a shit ton of money for charity, but remember, these guys are not a piece of meat, ladies. They're real boys with feelings." He waggles his finger to the crowd. "If you're bidding tonight, please come up to the front of the stage."

Harper grabs both Lily and me and hauls us through the crowd, placing us at the very front next to at least thirty other girls.

I spot mystery guy at the far right of the stage talking to another tall, broad-shouldered guy standing beside him.

"Okay, before we get started, a few rules. This is an auction, so if you'd like to bid, raise your paddle. If you raise it and you win, you pay the donation before leaving. Your date with the player starts as soon as the auction ends. That means he's all yours for the next six hours… wherever you crazy kids end up. No takebacks either. Thanks to John Ryan from last year, I've got to add that." He shakes his head. "Now, let the fun begin. We're going to introduce each player, tell you a little bit about them, and then they're going to mingle in the crowd briefly before the actual bidding begins."

Harper's fingers close around my wrist, tugging me against her side, and I can feel the excitement radiating off her.

I rake my teeth over my bottom lip to bite back my smirk, keeping my attention on the stage as the first few guys are announced. With each introduction, there's a new song played as they make their way down the line of girls waiting to bid on them, and I wonder what mystery guy's will be?

"Okay, now he's *hot*," Harper says dreamily as a stocky guy with a full beard that doesn't hide his bright smile walks out.

Damien.

Football player. His dog is his best friend, and he enjoys working out.

Cute, but… *pass.*

Yeah, the guys so far have been attractive, but no one has caught my attention the way mystery guy has.

And if I'm bidding on anyone tonight, it's going to be him.

"Yeah, he's cute. Bid on him!" I say to Harper.

She looks over at him, then back at me, her gaze shifting as she tries to decide. Ultimately, she shakes her head. "No, I think I want *that* guy down there."

Her pale-pink-tipped finger points toward the end of the stage, where a tall guy with buzzed blond hair stands, his lips tightened in a scowl as if he's not interested at all in being here.

Of course. Harper has a thing for broody assholes, so this absolutely checks.

"Lil, what about you, you gonna bid on anyone?"

Her eyes widen in what I can only describe as sheer panic as she shakes her head animatedly. "Uh… no. No way. *Definitely* not."

"You sure? That guy over there looks like he's definitely your type," I tease.

Another adamant headshake. She'd probably throw the paddle on the floor if Harper wouldn't pick it up and bid on someone for her. "Nope. Just here to watch and supervise you two. Someone has to keep an eye on you."

7

I grin with a nod and loop my arm around her shoulders, pulling her into me. My cheek presses against hers, and she laughs when I snake my tongue out and try to lick her.

"Love you, Lily pad. Don't worry, we'll save the corruption for another night."

Several of the guys make their way down the line to us, and a few dance with us, grab our hands, and spin us around. One guy drops to his knees in front of Lily, and I swear to god, I think she might actually faint on the floor of the Kappa house.

Fortunately for her, Kappa's president hurries it along and saves her from further mortification.

And finally, it's mystery guy's turn.

He saunters unhurriedly toward the middle of the stage, pulling at the loose-knotted tie around his neck, a mixture of pink and black that seems to make his skin even more tan in the dim light.

God, he is *so* fucking hot.

And although I'm blatantly aware of that, I don't want to seem too interested because that is not my style, so I sip my drink and feign the slightest amount of boredom as the Kappa president introduces him.

"Next up, we have Davis Guidry. He's a sophomore and is a pitcher for the Hellcats Baseball team. He considers himself a complete catch and the kind of guy who knows exactly what he wants."

Davis.

My fingers tighten around the paddle in my hand as I roll my lips together. His song?

"Yeah" by Usher.

I don't know the first thing about him, but somehow, I find myself thinking that it fits him. The cocky, assured swagger that he possesses. The flirty tilt of his lips. His molten irises that can only be described as bedroom eyes.

He makes his way toward the line of girls waiting to bid, starting at the opposite end from where I'm standing, and I expect him to take his time, charming each of them as the guys have before him, but no.

In the blink of an eye, he's made it to me, and he wastes no time dipping his head forward as his large hand lands on my hip, tugging my body against him.

His lips brush against the shell of my ear, and he whispers, "Gonna be real disappointed if you're not the highest bidder tonight, beautiful."

God, his *voice*.

It's low and raspy, a delicious baritone that has heat pooling in my belly and the crowd around us drowning out.

It's the first time in my life I've had such an immediate visceral reaction to a guy, let alone a stranger. My pulse is racing just from the brief interaction, and it surprises me.

He's surprised me.

With a wink and a slow, filthy lick of his lips that sets

my body on fire, he walks off, my gaze trailing on the tight slacks on his ass.

"Oh my god. What did he say?" Harper whisper-yells the moment he's out of earshot. "Tell me!"

I can't stop the smile flitting to my lips as I drain the last of my drink and turn toward her, "He said he's going to be disappointed if I'm not the one who wins him tonight."

"So does that mean you're going to bid on him?" Harper asks excitedly.

"I'm not just going to bid on him, Harp. I'm going to *win*."

chapter two

Zara

"Passenger Princess"— Nessa Barrett

"We'll start the bidding at $50 for Davis Guidry! Who's going to win OU's favorite ladies' man? Oh, we've got one over there, annnnd another!" Kappa's president yells into the microphone.

I raise the paddle to bid... and so does nearly every other girl in front of the stage.

I'm not surprised. I knew that this guy would be tonight's hottest commodity, and I love a challenge.

My gaze finds Davis's, and he smirks, arching a dark brow as if to say, *What are you waiting for?*

Things are moving at breakneck speed, bidding rising to two hundred and fifty bucks within a handful of seconds. I keep raising my paddle as the bidding continues to escalate, my gaze locked with his the entire time. Already growing tired of the back-and-forth bids, I step forward and raise my paddle in the air with finality. "A thousand dollars."

The crowd around us goes wild, a symphony of cheers and catcalls, and I smirk, dragging my gaze back to Harper and Lily. They both fall into my side, linking our arms together and giggling with me.

I said I was going to win, and I don't *ever* say anything that I don't mean.

"Oh, shit. Alright, going once... going twice," Kappa's president says to the room, and no one else raises to bid. "And *sold* for one thousand dollars to this gorgeous girl right here!"

When Davis's eyes find me, I grin and bring my fingers to my lips, blowing him a flirty kiss. He lifts his fist and closes it around the air as if he's catching it from across the stage.

The auction continues, and Harper ends up bidding on grumpy guy toward the end. Lily, of course, doesn't bid on anyone despite both of us trying to get her to try for the shy ginger-haired guy that we caught her secretly eying.

Rookie Mistake

"Let's go to the bathroom so we can touch up our makeup?" I say once the auction is over.

Harper nods. "Yes, please! I've had to pee for like an hour, but I didn't want to miss anything."

I reach for Lily's hand, and she follows closely behind Harper as we make our way through the crowded frat house. The lights are still low and the music even louder now that the auction has ended. It's hot and humid with the sea of bodies crammed into such a small space.

When we make it to the bathroom, there's a short line, but thankfully, it moves quickly, and soon, we squeeze inside and lock the door behind us.

I immediately move toward the full-length mirror next to the bathtub and pull my favorite lipstick from my purse.

"I love that dress on you, Zar," Lily says from where she's sitting on the counter. "Princess Polly?"

After I finish reapplying my signature red lips, I turn to her and nod with a smile. "Yep. It was on sale too."

"Honestly surprised your *warden* let you out of the house wearing that tonight, babe. Or that he'd even *let* you come to the Kappa auction," Harper mutters, walking to the sink to wash her hands.

The warden being my stupidly overprotective older brother, Oliver, whom I unfortunately live with.

He takes protective and overbearing to a whole new level.

Groaning, I nod. "He's driving me fucking nuts. I told him that I'm an adult, and it's time for him to stop suffocating me and that I don't need a babysitter, but if anything, it only makes him more crazy knowing that I'm not going to listen."

Of course, when he found out I'd be here tonight, he gave me a lecture and forbade me from coming. Especially after he saw me wearing my new satin black minidress that's backless save for the thin corset straps.

And while I love my brother and appreciate that he wants to look out for me, I seriously cannot handle the suffocation.

The constant fighting with him like he's my father and I'm a petulant child that isn't following his orders is honestly exhausting.

"Did he break out the ruler?" Lily asks, amusement twinkling in her pale azure eyes, her white teeth flashing as she grins. "To measure again?"

"Nope, but I would've punched him in the balls if he did."

Harper whips around. "He did *not* try to measure your dress."

I nod. "He did! He's losing it. Seriously. If I have to come crash in your dorm, you know why. I swear, I don't put it past him to put a tracker on me or something. Anyway, we ready?"

Nodding, Harper takes one last peek into the small mirror above the sink, smoothing her blonde hair down, then helps Lily off the counter, and together, we walk back out to the party.

"Why do you think that Oliver has been acting like this since you got to OU?" Lily asks, bringing the conversation back to my brother.

"I honestly don't know. It's like he and my dad both think I'm incapable of making my own decisions or making good choices since I'm not straight and narrow the way Ollie is. Sure, I've never been perfect, but then again, like who is? All I know is that I am done thinking about it. I refuse to let him ruin the vibe tonight."

It's already been a fantastic night, and the last thing I want to do is let the same exhausting fight with him fuck up my energy.

Law of attraction.

Something I live by.

Once we head to the back of the house, where the guys have set up a makeshift table to handle the auction closeout, I hand over my black Amex and take care of the donation before scanning the room for my date.

"Okay, so I'm going to head out with... Roman," Harper says, suddenly appearing at my side once more. She glances at her date, then drags her gaze back to me. "Your phone's charged and you have your location on, right?"

"Wow, you know, you sound *exactly* like Lil right now."

Lily shakes her head with a small, exasperated sigh

when Harper barks out a laugh. "Hopefully that means that you're *both* learning something from my constant mothering."

I nod. "Of course I am, Lil. Phone's charged, I've got my pepper spray, and my location is always on. Don't talk to strangers, and don't end up on a true crime podcast. No problem."

"Okay, I'm going to head back to the dorms. Call me if you need anything, okay?" she says before wrapping her arms around me and pulling me in for a tight hug.

Harper hugs me next, dropping a kiss against my cheek. "Have so much fun! You better call me as soon as you get home and tell me every single detail. Love you."

Once my girls have left, I grab another drink from the kitchen and then walk back toward the now empty stage. It doesn't take me long to spot Davis with his broad shoulder pressed against the wall, his hands tucked into the pockets of his black slacks, wearing a lazy, playful grin.

"A *thousand* dollars…" he murmurs when I come to a stop directly in front of him, my chin tilted to look up into his whiskey-colored eyes. "A lot of money for just one night."

My shoulder lifts in a shrug. "Guess you'd better make it worth my while, then, huh?"

A blaze of heat flares in his eyes, and my pulse races, my skin buzzing with anticipation.

His grin widens into a smile that shows two perfectly straight rows of teeth. "Seems a bit unfair that you know my name and I don't know yours. Think I should probably know the name of the girl I'm going to take on the best date of her life tonight."

"Mmm. Big talk for a guy who had to resort to an *auction* to get said date in the first place." I hold his gaze as I bring my cup to my lips and take a sip to hide my smile. Once I swallow down the heady alcohol, I lift my hand and hold it between us. "Zara."

"*Zara,*" he repeats, rolling each syllable on his tongue in a way that I feel in my core. His rough, warm palm slides along mine, curving and shaking gently as he holds my gaze with that cocky grin. A brief, electric moment, arguably the most innocent thing in the world, and yet it feels like he's currently peeling this dress off my body with only his gaze.

I nod as his thumb sweeps along the back of my hand, and he steps closer until he's nearly pressed against me. "And what does the best date of your life look like, Zara?"

My teeth rake over my bottom lip as I mull over the question. I've never really given it a lot of thought, not till now anyway.

"Something spontaneous. Something crazy. *Wild.* A night I couldn't forget even if I tried."

His eyes search mine, and finally, he nods, his full

lips curving up. "I think I know just the thing, then. You wanna get out of here?"

Finally.

"Thought you'd never ask."

After a brief smile, his fingers intertwine with mine, and he turns, leading me through the crowd toward the exit.

I DIDN'T EXPECT to end up in an Uber on a spontaneous date with the hottest guy I've ever seen when I decided to go to the Kappa house tonight.

I wanted freedom. I wanted to live in the moment.

And I wanted *this*. This feeling.

The wild flutter of my pulse. The thrash of my heart in my chest and the erratic whispers of butterflies erupting in my stomach.

"Just so you know, if you're planning to kidnap me, my location is on, and my girls are basically the FBI," I tease as we ride down the highway, the darkened city flying by. We're heading away from campus, and my curiosity is piqued.

He chuckles. "You bought *me*, remember? Maybe it's *you* with the nefarious plans to kidnap me and steal my virtue."

"Little ole me?"

"Mhmm." He reaches out, sweeping the rough pad of his finger along the small tattoos on my fingers. "I like these. You have any more?"

I glance down at my tattoos, nodding. "A... few. I got most of them over the summer. Mostly in places you can't see."

I don't miss the way his gaze flares, even in the darkened back seat. "Yeah? I'd love to see. Big, big fan of self-expression."

My laugh echoes throughout the back seat, and I nod. "I bet. Do you auction yourself off at the Kappa house often?"

"Only when it's for charity. Find yourself bidding on strangers for dates often?"

"Fair." I laugh.

I'm honestly having entirely too much fun going back and forth with him, and part of me doesn't want our ride to wherever it is we're going to be over.

"You a freshman?" he asks as he lifts his hand and drags his long fingers through his hair, pushing it off his face, giving me a glimpse of his deliciously chiseled jaw and strong, corded throat.

"Yeah, I am."

He nods, a smile playing on his lips. "Thought so. What's your major?"

"Musical composition."

"Wow." His brow arches. "And... what exactly is that?"

It's the same question that pretty much everyone asks when I tell them I'm majoring in composition, so I'm not surprised.

"The easy answer? Creating music. I play piano, and I write my own music. I'd like to maybe do it for someone else one day." I shrug. "I don't know, maybe it'll change, but I've been playing piano for as long as I can remember."

"That's awesome. So that's why you've got the music notes?" he asks, glancing down at my fingers again.

"Mhmm." I nod, wiggling them against the seat. "The slanted pound sign means sharp, and this one means flat. It's what a composer will use when determining the pitch of the music."

Davis nods as I speak, sweeping his finger absentmindedly over the dark ink on my pale skin.

I'm surprised by how genuinely interested he seems to be as I explain the meaning behind my tattoos. Most guys have zero interest in things like this.

"Cool. Well, maybe you can play for me one day. Maybe after I get my first tattoo."

"I don't know, I'm pretty sure the auction rules say only one night. I'm a big rule follower," I respond cheekily with a flash of a smile.

"Yeah? For some reason, I had you pegged as a girl

who wanted to do anything but follow rules. Guess I was wrong."

Before I can respond, our Uber turns into a packed parking lot and stops at the entrance of a black brick building that looks sketchy as shit, to say the least.

My gaze snaps to Davis, and I see that he's smirking.

Amusement shines in his eyes as he thanks the driver and reaches past me to curve his fingers over my door handle. I get a whiff of his cologne, and my mouth nearly waters.

God, he smells incredible.

Not only is he hot and has a fun personality to match, but he smells like he walked out of an Armani catalog.

"Ladies first."

I probably should question why we're at what looks like a dive bar in the middle of nowhere, but my curiosity outweighs the cautious, rational part of me.

What little exists.

My chunky combat boots crunch on the gravel as I step out, tucking my purse on my shoulder and glancing around the parking lot.

There are people loitering outside of the entrance that look like they're from *Sons of Anarchy*, some standing, some leaning along motorcycles with tall handlebars. Nearly everyone is wearing leather and bandanas, and that's when it hits me.

Turning to face Davis, who's just closed the car door

behind him, I say, "*Outlaw Oasis*. You brought me to a biker bar?"

The dimple in his cheek pops as he nods. "Yep."

Holy shit.

Well, this night just got *a lot* more interesting.

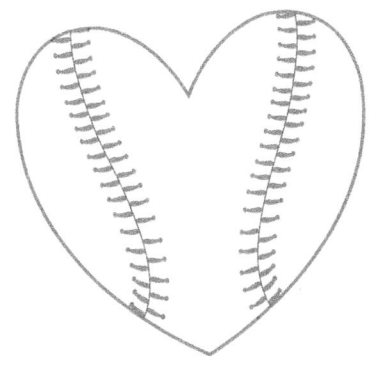

chapter three
Davis

"Ain't No Rest For The Wicked"— Cage The Elephant

Zara asked for spontaneous, and I'm pretty fucking sure there's nothing more spontaneous than a night of karaoke at a biker bar after buying me in an auction at a frat house.

But, then again, the night is still young and the possibilities endless.

Her pretty, bright red lips are parted in surprise, and I have to stop myself from reaching out and dragging my thumb along that plump bottom lip.

We've been dancing around each other since I first laid eyes on her in the Kappa house, and there's nothing more that I want right now than to taste to see if she's as delicious as she looks.

"It's karaoke night. Seemed like something *wild and fun*," I say, repeating her earlier words back to her. "Unless… you'd rather do something a little less… *crazy*?"

Her piercing green eyes narrow as her brow arches, and she shakes her head. "Nope. Obviously, you had no way of knowing this, but I actually karaoke at the Outlaw Oasis all the time. I'm a regular."

"Oh? That so?"

She nods. "Yeah. Is this your first time? *So* cute."

A laugh rumbles from my chest.

This fucking girl.

She's a breath of fresh air, and I'm desperate for another inhale, like an addict ready for their next hit.

When I saw her standing there across the room in that tiny black dress with those combat boots and bright red lips, I couldn't take my eyes off her.

I watched as she tossed her head back, her dark, midnight-black hair falling near her waist as she laughed at something her friend said, and fuck, I was *enthralled*.

It took me by surprise because it was the first time I'd ever felt such a... pull to a girl before. As sappy as it sounds, I was drawn to her, like a fucking magnet or something.

And I had to have more than just a glimpse in a crowded room.

I probably would've got down on my knees for her in front of everyone if she asked and not thought twice about it.

"C'mon, I'll show you around," she says with a smirk as she laces her fingers in mine and pulls me toward the entrance. "You know, since I've been here *so* often."

Something tells me this girl would match me toe to toe no matter what I threw at her, and that's so goddamn hot.

I'm not sure if it's the fact that I'm being dragged through the front door by a girl that's half my size or the fact that we *clearly* are not regular patrons of this establishment, but it has everyone's attention on us.

Probably a mixture of both.

The inside of the crowded bar is dark, with the same concrete-colored as the exterior, lit mostly by neon signs along the walls and dim fixtures hanging above the well-used pool tables. There's a small dance floor that faces the stage, where someone's belting out a fucking *horrible* rendition of "Ain't No Rest for the Wicked."

Zara whips to face me, her emerald eyes bright with

excitement. "Yesss. I fucking love this song! Let's dance." She lifts her hands above her head while her gaze stays locked on mine, pulling her plump bottom lip between her teeth, her hips beginning to sway to the beat. My mouth goes fucking dry.

She curls her finger in a come-hither motion, then slides her palms down the front of her body, rolling her hips with each pulse of the beat. The tight dress hugging her curves inches higher on her creamy thighs, and I bite back a groan.

I'm most *definitely* fucked.

"C'mon. Dance with me, *Loverboy*," she whispers as she steps closer and wraps her fingers around the loose tie on my neck, slowly tugging me toward her.

Yep.

Fucked.

"You're trouble, you know that?" I murmur. My hand splays along the curve of her hip, the smooth satin of her dress gliding beneath my palm as I move it to her lower back and yank her forward until she's flush against my front. My gaze drops to the hint of dark ink that peeks out from between her tits, trailing down her chest. Her nipples are taut and pebbled against the satin. "*So* much fucking trouble."

"Yeah, well, what's life without a little trouble? Makes things so much more fun."

In a beat, she turns, my arm still hooked around her waist as she rocks her ass against my dick, which is hardening by the second. My palm splays along her lower stomach, fisting in the material of her dress when her body rolls against mine, pulling a choked groan from me.

Her head drops back against my chest, and her eyes fall shut as we move together, in sync with the beat pulsing around us.

I feel her hand slide over the top of mine on her stomach, intertwining our fingers, and then she slowly drags it up her body over the flat expanse of her stomach to her rib cage until my hand rests along the curve of her tit. An inch higher and I could cup it in my hand, feeling the weight, rolling her taut nipple between my fingers until she cries out.

I dip my head to her ear. "You're playing with fire. I'm two seconds from bringing you into the bathroom and seeing if you taste as good as you look, *Trouble*. I've been dying to since the moment I saw you in that crowd." I sweep my thumb along the sensitive underside of her breast, causing her breath to hitch and my dick to twitch in my slacks.

Zara turns, her eyes shining with heat, a smirk toying with her pretty red lips as she trails a finger down the exposed part of my chest. "I came here for karaoke and drinks, Loverboy. Sorry."

My lips curve as I sweep a hand toward the stage. "Then, by all means, *Trouble*, lead the way."

I watch as she tosses me a smile and then turns and

walks toward the bar, her curvy hips swaying with each step. She's all of five foot two, but those legs go on for fucking days, and I want to put them over my shoulders while I fuck the shit out of her until she screams.

When I make it over to the long reclaimed wood bar, she's laughing with the bartender, who looks to be in his sixties with a haggard, white beard that reaches the middle of his chest. He's wearing a leather cut on top of a faded black T-shirt with a bandana covered in flames around his head.

"What's your poison?" Zara asks.

I shrug. "What's yours?"

Raking her teeth over her bottom lip, she turns back toward the bartender. "Two shots of Fireball, please, Ernie."

The bartender, apparently *Ernie*, nods with a wink that crinkles the corners of his eyes. "You got it, gorgeous."

Once he walks down to the opposite side of the bar, I lean forward, dipping my lips to her ear. "How'd you pull that off?"

She's a freshman, so obviously not old enough to buy a shot at the bar, yet the bartender didn't bat an eye when she ordered.

She stares up at me through thick, dark lashes and lifts her hand, flashing an ID between her fingers. "Graduation gift from my cousin Jeremiah."

"Ah. I knew you weren't a rule follower."

"Rules are boring, Loverboy." She laughs as she slides onto the barstool in front of her, then tucks her ID back in her purse. "And boring is *not* fun."

I slide onto the stool beside her just as Ernie returns, sliding two shot glasses full of amber-colored alcohol across the bar to us.

"Thanks, Ernie."

"Anytime, doll. Holler if you need me."

Zara nods, then reaches for the shot and lifts it in the air, offering me a playful smirk. "To spontaneous dates with strangers."

"And… to girls called Trouble," I add, clinking the glass against hers.

Together, we toss back the alcohol. It sears its way down my throat like it's forging actual fucking fire, and I slam the glass back onto the bar with a shake of my head.

"Fuck, that burns," I sputter. "You *like* that shit? I think I'd rather have a lobotomy."

She nods, and her tongue darts out, dragging along her lower lip, capturing the leftover liquid. "Don't be a baby. It's not *that* bad."

My gaze narrows. "Yeah? Let's do another, then."

I'm calling her bluff and wondering if she'll bite.

"Let's," she smarts back.

And that is exactly how, twenty minutes later, we're four shots and two drinks deep, well past tipsy and on our way to drunk. Two shots ago, we decided that we'd play a game... trying to guess each other's favorite things, and the loser has to drink.

Needless to say, I think she's cheating, and I just can't figure out how.

"Okay, okay," she breathes, leaning closer and placing her palms along my knees. "What's my favorite animal?"

"Fuuuuuck. Let me think. I feel like this should be easy, but fuck. The possibilities." I drag my hand through my hair, pushing it off my face as I start reciting a list of animals in my head. I'm absofuckinglutely losing this shit, but I'm getting to know her, so I'll take it. "Fuck it. Panda?"

A giggle bubbles out of her as she shakes her head, rolling her lips together. "Nope. Drink up."

I lift my half-empty glass of beer to my lips and take a gulp.

"It's a naked mole rat."

My eyes widen, and I groan. "What the fuck, Zara? I would have never gotten that shit! A mole rat? Jesus Christ."

"I know." She laughs. "But it's true. They're so cute and hairless! I want one. I swear, it's true."

I reach for the seat of her barstool and haul her toward me until she's nestled between my spread legs. "I think you're just trying to get me drunk, Trouble. You wouldn't do that, would you?"

Her lip slides between her teeth, and she shakes her

head, leaning forward and sliding her hands up my thighs, dangerously close to my cock. "Of course not. You're just actually terrible at this game."

"Or... maybe you're just cheating."

"I would never. Scout's honor." She smirks while reaching for my tie, fingering the fabric and holding my gaze as she leans closer. But when the song suddenly changes and they do an open call for karaoke, she halts, her eyes going wide as she leans back. "Oh, hell yesssss, finally. Let's go."

In a second, she's sliding off the barstool, a laugh rumbling from me as she drags me to the stage, then pushes me down into a rickety chair right in the front row.

Front and fucking center.

I sit back, crossing my arms over my chest as I watch her walk onto the stage and whisper something in the MC's ear, who nods and smiles at her before passing her the microphone. The music cuts as she takes her spot, and while the crowd that's gathering is less than enthusiastic about the music stopping, they perk up when they see Zara in the center of the stage with a sexy grin playing on her pretty red lips.

Lips that I'm desperate to taste. To feel wrapped around my cock.

I've spent the entire night staring at those lips and imagining what they'll feel like when I can finally kiss her.

Which I plan on doing the second she gets off that stage.

"This song is for the guys who love a little bit of *trouble*. Specifically, the one sitting right there." She points directly at me, and I laugh, shaking my head as the people around me cheer. Someone claps me on the shoulder, and her grin only widens as the music begins to play again.

"Trouble" by Camyilo plays through the speakers, and Zara starts singing, shaking her hips to the beat as she belts out the raspy, low notes.

I cover my mouth, laughing as she spins around the stage singing, but if anything, it just makes me find her that much more attractive.

The fact that she truly doesn't give a shit what anyone thinks. She's not trying to impress me, or anyone, for that matter.

She's fucking wild. She's fun. She's confident and sexy and fuck. I like it.

I'm completely under her spell, and honestly, I can't remember a time I had so much fun.

She flips her long, dark hair over her shoulder as she saunters off the stage with the microphone toward me, stopping between my spread legs. I reach for her, unable to stop myself, sliding my hands along the soft, exposed skin along the back of her thighs, gently pulling her toward me. She doesn't miss a beat as her fingers slide into my hair, and she tugs roughly at the long strands.

Her head dips, and suddenly, she's a breath away from my lips, a single fucking breath, singing a song that I'm no longer even listening to because I can't focus on anything other than her blown pupils and the fact that I'm about to have a hard-on in front of an entire bar full of bikers.

The tips of my fingers tighten around the back of her thighs, digging into her creamy skin.

The song ends, and the entire room erupts in a cheer for a show that I don't think any of us anticipated happening before it started.

Zara's chest heaves as she sucks in a breath, her eyes dropping to my lips and lingering before she stands and offers the crowd a small wave, then hands the microphone back to the person in charge of karaoke.

This was a fucking religious experience.

One I'm going to fuck my hand to more times than I care to admit.

I don't know what it is about this girl, but I'm in so fucking deep.

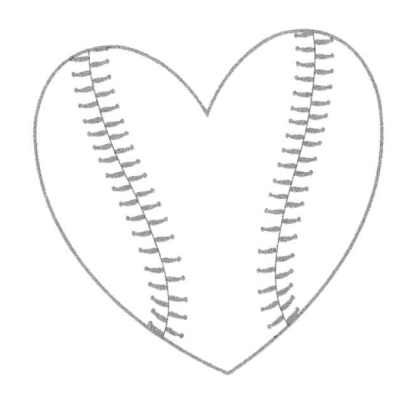

chapter four

Davis

"Trouble"— Camylio

When I stand from the chair, Zara slips her hand in mine and starts to tug me toward the bar, calling back over her shoulder, "I need a drink, a shot… *something.*"

I don't need to hear her say it to know exactly what she's feeling.

Shit, that just felt like the hottest foreplay of my

fucking life, and my dick's still hard despite my attempt at tucking it into the waistband of my briefs.

"How about you pick this time," she says when we get back to the bar, and she flags down Ernie. "Since Fireball isn't your thing."

"Alright. What about… tequila?"

She shrugs, offering me a smile before telling Ernie, "Two shots of tequila with lime, please."

I notice when she turns to face the bar that the strap of her dress has fallen, so I lift my hand and slide it back in place, letting the pads of my fingers sweep along her heated skin.

A seemingly innocent movement, but she shivers in response, dragging her eyes to mine and swallowing roughly.

Time slows, and for a moment, we stay just like that, my fingers sweeping along the soft skin of her shoulder, her vibrant green eyes holding mine.

"Here you go, darlin'," Ernie's gravelly voice interrupts from the other side of the bar. We both turn to see the shot glasses of tequila he's sliding to us, along with a set of limes.

Zara thanks him, giving him a saccharine smile as she grabs the tequila and lime and turns back toward me. "Okay, Loverboy, drink up."

"Yes, ma'am."

I pick the shot up, clinking the shot glass against

hers, and we toss them back, immediately sucking on the lime afterward.

Zara's nose scrunches, and her lips pucker as the lime juice runs down her chin and drips onto her neck. "Jesus, that's more bitter than I expected. Ugh, shit, it's everywhere."

"Yeah, looks like a mess," I murmur, leaning in, "Let me be a good boy and help you clean it up."

Heat flares in her eyes, her pupils wide and blown, her lips parting.

Lowering my mouth to her neck, I drag my tongue along the rivulet of juice, licking and sucking every drop off her skin.

And fuck, for something that's supposed to taste sour, it tastes so goddamn sweet.

"Davis," she breathes, her hands flying to the front of my shirt and fisting in the fabric.

I love hearing her tease me by calling me Loverboy, but I love hearing her moan my name even more. I want nothing more than to hear her screaming it while I eat her, fuck her, worship her.

Her cheeks are flushed and her eyes heavy-lidded when I pull back, giving her a cocky grin.

"Wha—"

"God, will you shut up and kiss me already? I'm tired of waiting," she murmurs, colliding into me and sliding her arms around my neck. Her fingers tangle in the hair at my nape, those pointy, black nails scraping against my skin and causing *me* to fucking shiver.

Thank fuck.

I slide my hand to the back of her neck and pull her forward, my lips crashing with hers roughly, hours of pent-up want exploding between us, making the air heavy and thick. My tongue sweeps into her parted lips, and she whimpers when I stroke it against hers the same way that I would fuck her.

Slow and deliberate, I take my time tasting her, committing it to memory.

Hot and wet. A frantic, desperate tangle of tongues that doesn't feel like enough, like it could never be enough.

This kiss is fucking *dangerous.*

It's the kind of kiss that makes a guy do stupid shit. A kiss he'd lay it all on the line for.

My pulse races when her hands slip beneath the loose fabric of my shirt, the muscles tightening as she rakes her nails along my abs. She whimpers, soft and so fucking sweet, when I bring my hand to her hair and fist it in response, tipping her head back and angling her mouth to kiss her deeper, swallowing down every little noise, every mewl.

Every fucking *breath.*

Her lips move from mine for the briefest fleeting moment, and I feel her whispering breathlessly against

Rookie Mistake

my mouth, "I want you. Please, get me out of here. Right now."

I pull back, peering down at her as her plea washes over me. She has no fucking idea just how badly I want her, but fuck, it was that easy to forget we're in a bar room full of people.

We're not exactly at the kind of place with many options for privacy, especially for all of the things I want to do to her.

And apparently, I've got all of those things written on my face because she seems to know exactly what I'm thinking. Her eyes bounce around the bar, drifting over the crowd of people and around the room until it lands on the darkened hallway, and her brow lifts, an unspoken question passing between us.

Fuck it.

"Let's go," I say, grabbing her hand and weaving her fingers in mine as I turn and guide us through the crowded bar.

I have no fucking clue where I'm going; all I know is I want Zara alone. The hallway at the back of the bar is dark and small, with boxes of liquor piled everywhere and a few random photos along the walls. Zara's hand tightens in mine as I lead her further past the bathrooms to where I see a set of doors at the end.

The door to the right has a sign that says Office on it, so I guide her to the one on the left and try the knob.

39

Thank fuck, it opens. I hurriedly pull us both inside and shut the door before someone sees us.

It's dark inside the room, with only thin slivers of moonlight filtering through the window, but enough that I can make out what's inside. This must be where they store the extra alcohol and supplies. There are boxes stacked around the room, and I can see the glint of glass bottles reflecting in the moonlight.

It's slightly musty and damp in here, but at least we're alone. The only sound is the faint thump of music coming from the bar, the bass vibrating the walls slightly as it pours through the speakers.

Zara turns to face me, her dark lashes fanning along her cheeks as she drags her eyes to mine, and I can't wait another fucking second to touch her.

I curve my palm along her hip and close the distance between us until she's pressed against my front. Her breath hitches at the contact, a breathy little noise escaping her lips that shoots directly to my dick and nearly causes my brain to short-circuit.

"Finally alone, Trouble," I murmur. "Now, what are you going to do about it?"

Her lips tilt and her eyes flare as she lifts her chin and ghosts her lips along mine. The smallest brush of contact that has me fucking dizzy with desperation to taste her, touch her, fuck her until she's screaming my name.

"What I've been waiting to do all night," she whispers against my skin, kissing the corner of my mouth softly at the same time she slides her hands beneath my shirt and brushes the tips of her fingers along my lower abs.

That's all it takes for the tightly wound cord to snap.

My hand slides into her hair as she slams her lips against mine and moans hungrily into my mouth, the sound slipping into my bloodstream like a hit of the most potent drug, and I'm fucking gone. When her tongue sweeps into my mouth, I lift her off her feet and carry her to the stack of boxes behind her, placing her at the edge as I step between her parted thighs.

Her hips roll against my aching cock with every brush of our tongues, and I can feel the heat of her pussy through my slacks as she grinds against me.

There's nothing slow or explorative about the way we're moving together.

I've wanted her since the moment I laid eyes on her, and this chemistry, this electric current of tension between us, has been a constant buzzing hum.

Tearing my lips from hers, I kiss along the edge of her jaw, grazing and nipping at her heated skin. I soothe the bite with my tongue before trailing a wet, searing path down her neck, tasting the sweet, salty remnants of tonight on her.

"I've been thinking about this all night. Tasting you. Seeing those pretty little red lips smeared from being kissed by me," I mumble against her skin. Her fingers thread into my hair as I continue my path lower, tugging roughly at the strands. The bite of pain, a mixture with heady pleasure, is an unexpected surprise.

My lips trail along her collarbone, down her chest, until I pull back to admire the taut, pebbled little peaks of her nipples as they press against the fabric of her dress.

I lift my eyes to hers, drinking in the flush of her cheeks and her swollen, parted lips as she peers down at me with heavy-lidded eyes framed in thick, dark lashes.

She's a fucking vision bathed in pale moonlight, and I wish I had more time so I could properly see her. Strip her bare and take my time appreciating every inch of her.

"Then be a *good boy* and get on your knees for me." Her words are a breathless pant.

I bring my thumb to her mouth, dragging the rough pad of it over her bottom lip, smearing the red on her lips slightly.

Her gaze darkens as she sucks my finger into her mouth and swirls her tongue along the tip just the way I imagine she would with my cock.

Something I'd do just about anything to see right now.

"This mouth," I rasp darkly. "One day, I'm going to fuck it. Then, we'll see just how much of a brat you are when your throat is stuffed full of my cock."

Smirking around my finger, she bites down roughly

on the tip, her eyes lighting up with something I can't exactly place.

Excitement? Maybe even a challenge.

Fuck yeah, I knew Zara would be the kind of girl to match me toe to toe, and the flickering desire in her eyes proves it.

I pull my thumb free and do just as I'm told, dropping to my knees between her legs, keeping my gaze focused on hers as I run my palms slowly up the top of her thighs, inching her dress higher.

Her legs fall open as the dress bunches at her hips, exposing the tiniest, barely there scrap of lace covering her pussy. I have to bite back a groan when I see the damp spot darkening the front of the fabric.

Fuck.

I haven't even touched her yet, and she's already soaked.

Sliding my arms beneath her thighs, I curve them around her hips and yank her to the edge, placing her legs over my shoulder as I brush the pad of my thumb over the wet lace. I dip my head and press my lips softly against her clit. Then, I flatten my tongue and drag it over the fabric, licking her through it.

I tug the lace aside with my fingers, exposing her pussy. Pretty and pink, glistening with her arousal, her swollen little clit peeks out, begging for my mouth.

My fingers trace the glistening seam of her pussy, coating them with her arousal. I spread her open and flick my tongue over her clit once, then again when her hips rock against my mouth, all while I watch her, taking in the way her breath hitches and she tosses her head back on her shoulders, sinking further into the wall behind her.

"Can you be a good girl and be quiet while I eat your pretty little pussy, Trouble?" I drag my finger through her wetness, circling her entrance but never pushing inside.

When she doesn't answer me, I pull my hand back and lightly slap her pussy. Just enough to get her attention.

Her eyes snap open and rake down to me, a look of surprise flickering in her eyes.

"Did you just... *spank* my pussy?

I smirk against her heated flesh. "Yeah, I did, and if we weren't in the back room of this fucking bar, I'd spank your ass the same way. Bad girls who are trouble need to be punished."

"God, you're so fucking hot, Davis."

Trailing my finger back up to her clit, I rub a soft, languid circle, watching as her eyes flutter shut. "Answer my question. Can you be quiet?"

After a beat, she nods, raking her teeth over her pillowy bottom lip.

Without wasting another second, I drag my tongue up her pussy from ass to clit, lapping at her.

Goddamnit, she tastes too fucking good, I want to drown in her.

My tongue circles her clit, flicking the tight little nub until she's rocking against my face, her fingers threaded in my hair, holding my mouth tightly to her.

"Fuck." A strangled moan tumbles breathlessly from her parted lips, and I pause, pulling back to look up at her.

I delve my tongue into her tight hole while I strum her clit with my thumb in quick, rough circles.

Zara seems to like a bit of pain with her pleasure, and fuck, there's nothing sexier.

If I thought she was breathtaking before? It doesn't hold a candle to the way she looks with my tongue buried in her pussy. Her dark lashes fan against her cheeks as she writhes, rubbing her pussy on my face unabashedly.

Seeing her cheeks flushed pink from pleasure makes me wonder if her skin would bloom the same way from my hands.

I slide two fingers inside of her while circling her clit with my tongue, and the moment I hook them up, she whimpers my name so fucking soft and sweet that I nearly come in my pants.

"Right there, yes. Yes. Yes," she chants. "*Please* don't stop."

As if there's anything in the fucking world that would stop me from devouring her.

Closing my lips around her clit, I fuck her harder with my fingers, stroking that spot until I feel her tightening around me.

"Coming. Oh god... Davis," she whimpers, panting, thrashing, as her fingers tighten in my hair.

The slick walls of her pussy clamp down on my fingers, and she comes wildly, tossing her head to the side as her entire body trembles. Her thighs snap shut, tightening around my head and holding me in place while she rides out her orgasm.

And I can't stop watching her, admiring how goddamn pretty she is.

My free hand slides up her stomach to tweak her pebbled nipples. I tug and pull, prolonging the orgasm until she's too sensitive.

It's over too quickly, leaving me aching for more.

She said she was trouble, and now I'm realizing just how fucking much I'm in.

chapter five

Zara

"ANGEL"— Toby Mai

I just had the best orgasm of my *entire* life.

Pressed against the wall in a storage room of a biker bar, my hands tangled in Davis's hair, my moans drowned out by the sound of a poorly sung rendition of "It's Raining Men," without a single moment of regret.

Not *one*.

In fact, I'm desperate for more from the guy who had

zero hesitation in dropping to his knees and devouring me like he was starving and I was his last meal.

Things probably would have gone further if it hadn't been for the last-call announcement made through the speaker system, letting everyone in the bar know it's closing time. I barely heard it through the wall over the erotic sound of Davis lapping at my pussy and the thundering beat of my heart.

"Fuck," he rasps, dropping his forehead against my stomach, his hot breath fanned over my overly sensitive core. "How the fuck is it already 2:00 a.m.?"

"You know what they say. Time flies when you're having fun."

His deep, hoarse chuckle vibrates my skin, and I exhale shakily. Every part of my body is still buzzing from his wickedly talented tongue and from the way tonight has felt.

My leg falls from his shoulder, combat-boot-clad foot sliding to the floor as he rises to his feet. His eyes darken as they wash over my body sagging against the boxes. "You're so goddamn pretty, Zara." Reaching for me, he drags his fingers down the center of my chest, where the ink stains my skin. "The prettiest thing I've ever seen in my goddamn life."

Teeth dragging over my bottom lip, I stare up at him as he lifts his hand and sweeps his thumb along the corners of my lip before placing his palm flat along the wall behind me.

His mouth lowers, so close to mine that I think he might kiss me again, but he doesn't.

He just hovers there, breathing me in and staring into my fucking soul with his dark, amber eyes.

"The bar's closing, and I know I should probably take you home, but I'm really not fucking ready for this night to be over, Trouble."

"Who says it has to?" I whisper, lifting my hands to his sides, where my fingers fist in the fabric of his wrinkled dress shirt, tugging him closer to me. "The night is still young, and we make the rules, Loverboy."

"Yeah?"

His dark brow lifts with the corner of his lip, a playful grin transforming his handsome face.

Every time he's offered that effortless grin tonight, a flurry of something foreign tugs low in my belly, and I want to chase that feeling, no matter where it leads.

And that's why this guy is dangerous.

Because chasing something fun, something temporary, is all that I'm after, but guys like Davis... they make you feel like there's more to be had under the surface, underneath all the pretty and shiny feelings that give you butterflies and make your heart race in your chest.

Nodding, I roll my lips together, contemplating my next words since they're as crazy as anything we've done tonight. "I know a place... if you're up for it."

"Would probably be up for anything if you were involved."

My head falls back against the wall as a giggle tumbles out of me. "You sure about that?"

Without hesitation, he nods. "Fuck yeah. Take me wherever you want, Trouble."

"WONDERLAND TATTOO?" Davis questions as he shuts the door to the Uber, dragging his gaze from the eccentrically painted studio over to me.

I smirk, popping a brow. "Still up for *anything*?"

His head shakes when he laughs, the long dark strands of his hair falling in his face, and my fingers itch to reach out and tangle through them.

"How about something to remember the best date of your life?" I add before he can answer.

I fully expect him to call my bluff. To end the night right here.

Not to grab my hand and thread those long, strong fingers through mine, tugging me against him until I can feel every hard, sharp ridge of his body.

Nor do I expect him to look down at me with those deep-amber, golden-flecked eyes, a boyish smirk on his lips, and shrug. "Fuck it, why not?"

"Really?" I ask, my tone full of surprise that makes his smirk spread into a smile.

"What? You didn't think I would?"

Well... no. Actually.

I thought he'd draw the line on this kind of spontaneity, but once again, he's surprised me, just the way he has all night.

I'm realizing how much Davis matches my energy. He's fun and full of life. He's reckless in the best kind of way. He doesn't back down, even when it seems crazy. He doesn't care about the outside noise and is perfectly content doing whatever makes him happy, and it's rare to find someone comfortable enough with themselves to enjoy that. It's so fucking hot.

When I walked into the Kappa house for the auction, I never would have guessed the night would end up how it has.

He's not at all something I expected.

Shrugging, I take a few slow steps backward toward the building, pulling him along with me, gaze trained on him. The parking lot is dark, with only a few low-lit streetlights scattered along the pavement. "Not really. I mean, you're a tattoo virgin. Are you sure you want to give it up here tonight, with me? Seems like a pretty big commitment for a first date."

"And who says I'm not a commitment kind of guy?" he hedges. "I might be an *only* commitment kind of guy."

I laugh as we come to a stop in front of the entrance, a heavy black door painted in theme with *Alice in Wonderland*'s Mad Hatter. The zany and dramatic cartoon features are painted with striking accuracy.

"Sorry, Loverboy, but I'm calling bullshit. I was there tonight, remember? I saw all of those girls ready to jump on you the second they secured their prize."

He nods at the same time his shoulder dips, stepping forward until I collide with the door behind me. "Maybe so, but it was over the second a pretty little thing in combat boots caught my eye. You know what I thought the moment I saw you?" His palm flattens on the door behind me, caging me in as his free hand lifts to the neckline of my dress, where it curves loosely around my small cleavage. His fingertips score along my heated skin, creating a symphony inside my rib cage. "I thought about how perfect you'd look on your knees, those red fucking lips stretched around my cock, taking me down your throat."

Oh god.

Heat pools in the place in my belly that has my core tightening, my clit throbbing with fierce desperation.

"I wanted you from the moment I laid eyes on you. I saw no one else. Only *you*, Trouble," he murmurs against my parted lips, still holding my gaze with an intensity that has my toes curling in the boots he seems to love so much. "Now, you wanna go in here and get a tattoo? Let's fucking go. But I need something before we do."

"What?"

My voice sounds as breathless as I feel, and the corner of his lip curves up.

"I need to kiss you because I've been fucking dying to since we left that bar, and I'll be a real good boy if I can taste those lips again before I give up my virginity to a stranger."

I can't help but toss my head back and laugh because, god, it's so fucking ridiculous, but it's also him, and I want that too.

"Are you asking for permission?"

His gaze darkens. "Do I need it?"

Every second of this banter between is driving me insane with need. I don't think I've ever been more turned on in my life.

"No," I whisper against his mouth, brushing my lips against his slightly as I lift onto my tiptoes and curve my arms around his neck. As if already a habit, my fingers tangle into the long hair at his nape, my fingernails lightly scraping along his scalp.

"So much fucking trouble" is all he says before he's kissing me, taking my mouth so possessively that a shiver dances down my spine. It's not only a kiss; it's an act of war, a proclamation of ownership that's like a brand along my lips. His tongue sweeps into my mouth, and he swallows every whimper, every stuttering exhale.

And then I feel his teeth grazing my lips as he pulls back and nibbles on them, sending a delicious shiver down my spine and goose bumps scattering along my flesh.

"You have no idea how badly I want to take you home, take you anywhere, and finish what we started, Zara. But if we do that, then we're not making it to this appointment." He drops his forehead against mine. "Tell me let's go inside and get these tattoos."

"I... Yes. Come on." I slip my fingers into his and turn to the door.

He's a perfect gentleman and holds it open for me, letting me step inside before he does. The door shuts behind him, and we look around the shop together.

Even though it's nearly three in the morning, Wonderland is still alive and full of people.

And honestly, I'd be more surprised if it wasn't. Of all the tattoo parlors in New Orleans, it's the best, no question.

Not only are their artists the most talented in the city, but the vibes and energy are unmatched.

Gracie, my artist and one of my favorite people, is the only person I'll ever let tattoo me. She's amazing, and I don't trust anyone else to put something permanent on my skin.

The parlor is spacious, an eclectic mix of dark blues,

purples, and black, adorned with a gothic, dark version of *Alice in Wonderland* told in murals on the wall. There's a shelf above the deep blue velvet couches with various statues of characters from the original movie.

"This place is fucking sick. You always come here to get your stuff done?" Davis asks as we stand side by side in the foyer, admiring the portraits along the walls.

I had no clue if he'd be down for this, but I texted Gracie as soon as we left the bar and asked her to squeeze us in for something super small and that I would owe her for life.

Thankfully, she loves me because she gave us her last slot.

I nod. "The girl who does my tattoos, Gracie, she's the artist on most of these. She owns the parlor with her twin brother, Grayson. I got my first tattoo with her and every one since. It's only been a few months, but she's stuck with me for life," I say as I reach up and drag my finger along a black-and-white portrait of a Roman statue. It's one of my favorite pieces she's ever done, and I always tell myself that I'm going to have her do something similar for my thigh piece that I'll eventually get.

"My favorite mural is this one."

Davis's gaze travels the length of mine to where I'm staring at a full wall mural of Alice skipping into a field of psychedelic mushrooms that glow under the black light they've installed in this room.

The detail is incredible, and the style is a total vibe.

"Mhmm. This is crazy good," he agrees, shoving his hands in the pockets of his slacks. "Should probably figure out what we're getting, yeah?"

I nod, scanning the room for Gracie's portfolio books. They're full of her art for when people need inspiration, and honestly, this will be the first spontaneous tattoo I've ever gotten. The rest of my tattoos have been planned, designs that I've wanted for a long time.

I spot the dark purple, leather-bound books on a table near her room, and I walk over, picking it up, then turn to face Davis.

"The grimoire for reckless, last-minute decisions." I grin, waving the large book in front of me. His dark brow furrows in confusion, so I add, "Gracie's portfolio book."

My gaze slides to the curve of his pillowy lips and the smallest hint of a dimple that appears right next to it on his cheek. It's hard to focus on anything other than how ridiculously sexy he looks leaned against the wall nonchalantly, hands shoved in his pant pockets, his dark hair tucked behind his ears as he looks at me with a heated stare that should not have as much of an effect on me as it does.

Crossing the room, I sit on the small velvet sofa and peer up at Davis. "Come on, Loverboy. Big decisions and *so* little time."

He chuckles, lowering himself into the seat beside me.

I open the book, pausing on the very first page and pointing to a hairless sphinx. "You should absolutely get this one. Cats feel like your thing."

"The fuck, Zara?" His laugh slides through my veins like the most addicting drug on the planet. "Pass. But this one..." His finger lands on a small bat. "This one might be the one."

When I roll my eyes and keep flipping absentmindedly through the book, he places a large hand over the pages.

"Nah, you know what. You want *spontaneous*?" He smirks from beside me, snapping the portfolio shut. "I pick yours. You pick mine. Spontaneous as it gets, baby."

My brow arches. "That seems like an absolutely terrible idea for your *first* tattoo."

"Why, you scared, *Trouble*? It's okay if you are. You can just say that." His back hits the plush velvet sofa, and he crosses his arms over his chest with that stupid shit-eating grin that makes the fluttering in my stomach become a hurricane that can't be quelled.

"I'm not scared," I scoff. "I just don't want you to regret it. They're forever, you know?"

"I'm starting to think *you're* the one with the commitment issues."

I roll my eyes again as a laugh falls from my parted

lips. "You've barely seen a fraction of the commitment on my body, Loverboy. The best ones are reserved for those who are lucky enough to get to see them."

His eyes darken at my retort, dropping briefly to my chest where the fabric of my satin dress hangs loosely, offering him the smallest view of cleavage and the dark ink staining my chest.

The way his gaze sweeps over my skin feels like a caress, as if he's using the rough pads of his fingers to memorize every inch without ever touching me.

Side by side on this sofa, his thick thigh pressed against mine, we're caught in a moment that feels too intimate to be surrounded by people in a tattoo parlor.

"You down, Trouble?" He rasps the question, but it feels like he's asking something else entirely, and I'm wound so tightly that it takes every ounce of restraint not to climb into his lap and finish what we started earlier.

God, I'm painfully horny, and one orgasm *obviously* wasn't enough. I'm not sure two would even come close.

"I'm not the kind of girl to back down from a challenge. I'm down," I murmur, reaching up and dragging my thumb along his bottom lip, smirking when his breath catches.

He has no idea just how much I *love* a challenge.

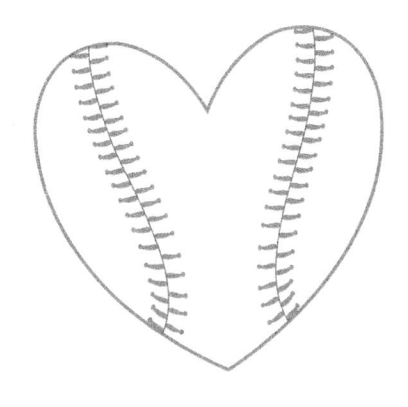

chapter six

Davis

"Teeth"— 5 Seconds of Summer

I might have forgotten to mention I'm not exactly the biggest fan of needles.

But then again, it's been nearly impossible to think about anything else besides how good her sweet little pussy tasted with my tongue buried inside of it. How pretty and pink she was, swollen and puffy from the scruff on my chin as I lapped at her greedy cunt. Or those little fucking whimpers she made when she was about to come, her thighs tightening around my head like a vise, the heel of her boots digging into my back when she finally did come, coating my face in her cum.

Fuck. My dick's getting hard again just thinking about it.

Zara is a goddamn fever dream, and I'm not ready to wake up.

I'm not ready for tonight to end, which is why I'm sitting in a tattoo chair with a needle digging into the skin beneath the waistband of my briefs.

The low, vibrating buzz of the tattoo gun pulls me from my thoughts, and I glance up at Zara sitting on the opposite side of the artist, her slender fingers intertwined with mine and a pretty smile on her bloodred lips.

I never knew how much I loved the color red until I stared at it on her lips all night.

Now, it just might be my *favorite* color.

"You okay?" she asks, leaning forward and placing her hand flat on my abdomen, then dropping her chin onto the top. Under the bright, fluorescent light of the tattoo parlor, I see the tiny gold flecks in her green-colored irises.

Holy shit.

They're beautiful.

I clear my throat and nod. "Mhm. All good. Doesn't hurt as bad as I thought it would. More like a beesting. Continuously."

Zara laughs. "It does, but not really pain, per se. It's the best therapy in the world. Think you'll get any more?"

"I dunno. Maybe?" My shoulder dips along the chair. "Honestly, I'm the kind of guy who lives for the moment. I never think too far ahead, and sometimes that's my downfall. But I like to live in the now. I'll worry about the rest later."

The needle hits a sensitive patch of skin, and I groan, "Fuck."

Her small hand tightens in mine, and she gives me a reassuring smile.

"The only way to live, if you ask me."

Thanks to her soft hand in mine, before I know it, the tattoo is done, and the artist is covering the art now inscribed on my lower abdomen.

I glance down at the gauze covering Zara's wrist that hides the tattoo I picked for her from view. She got hers first, and we agreed we would get our first looks together.

We walk over and stand near the door, peering at each other with stupid, silly grins on our faces. Once she peels back the gauze, she shakes her head. "Oh god." The tendrils of her low, smoky laugh seep through the air as she inspects the small tattoo on the inside of her wrist. "You would pick this. It's perfect." Her eyes lift to mine, and she shakes her head again, rolling those plump red lips together to stifle another laugh.

A little angel with a set of horns on the top of its head.

I knew the second I saw it this was it. A perfect combination of the girl I've grown to know tonight, even though I know I've only scratched the surface.

She's the perfect mixture of sweet and dirty, and lord fucking knows I want more of the small taste I got earlier.

"Kinda worried now, Loverboy. Not sure the one I picked is gonna measure up to yours, but I guess it's time for the moment of truth." Zara smirks, arching a dark brow as she steps forward and tugs the front of my shirt up, exposing abs that I'm really fucking glad I didn't let go over the summer just by the way her eyes are darkening as they drink me in.

Her fingers lightly trail along the muscles, dipping between the ridges and stroking lower. Lower and lower until her fingers slip beneath the waistband and ghost along the sensitive skin, all while those golden-flecked green eyes hold mine so tightly it feels like I can't breathe.

Fuck.

What *is* it about this girl?

What is it about her that makes the entire room drown out, and all I see is her?

How is it that we only just met tonight, yet it feels like we've known each other for years? There's an easiness between us, a familiarity that shouldn't exist, but somehow, it does.

"You nervous?" The playful smirk on her lips widens as my shoulder dips.

"Should I be?"

Those perfect lips roll together as she hides her smile, offering me a nonchalant shrug.

"I dunno. See for yourself, Loverboy." Her hands settle at my hips, and then she tugs me toward the floor-length mirror on the parlor wall.

Fuck, am I nervous?

Nah, nervous isn't it. It's *anticipation*.

It sparks down my spine like a current as she pulls off the bandage, exposing the dark ink, one simple but unforgettable word tattooed just below my hip bone.

Trouble.

"Now you'll always remember tonight," she murmurs, holding my gaze in the mirror, her bright eyes sparkling.

I turn to face her, my gaze dropping to her parted lips as my throat bobs, and I reach for her, sliding my hands along her jaw to tangle in the dark, silky strands at her nape.

"Yeah, that's the thing. Something tells me I'm never going to be able to forget tonight," I whisper against her mouth, each exhale from her lips an inhale that fills my lungs.

Just as I close my lips over hers, there's a loud throat

clearing behind us, and begrudgingly, I tear my lips away.

"Sorry, but we're closing. Don't care where ya go, but ya gotta get outta here," a tall guy with a long handlebar mustache says from the entryway of one of the tattoo rooms.

Zara giggles, burying her head in my chest, and I nod sheepishly. "Yeah, man, sorry. We're headed out."

After we pay for our tattoos, we bust out of the door like two teenagers who've just been caught making out, laughing the entire time.

Shit, tonight's been fun.

Unexpectedly something I didn't even know I was missing until now.

The sun's peeking out behind the clouds when we step out of the tattoo shop, rising over the horizon in shades of orange and gold.

"Damn, it's late. Or should I say… early?" I mutter, glancing over at Zara as we walk side by side through the parking lot. "I feel like tonight has passed so fast and yet slow all at the same time."

"I know exactly what you mean. I can't remember the last time I stayed up until the sun came up, let alone going to a biker bar, then getting a tattoo with a stranger."

I nod. I've never done this with anyone before, a spontaneous date, but definitely not a date that I don't want to end.

"My town house is just a few blocks up ahead," she says. "If you wanna walk me?"

Her pinky brushes against mine as we walk, and I don't hesitate to grab her hand, lacing my fingers through hers. We walk in the direction of her town house, and she tells me about her best friends. How they've been friends since they were kids and that they're all at OU together now.

Realization hits me with the force of a head-on collision at the fact that for the first time that I can ever clearly remember, I want to know more than just the surface of a girl.

I want to meet the friends she's talking about with the biggest smile on her face. I want to know what her favorite thing to order at a restaurant is. I want to hear her play her music. Who she is when all the layers are peeled away. I want to *know* her.

And that's as terrifying as it is thrilling to think about.

"This you?" I ask when we come to a stop outside of an older, two-story brick building with burgundy shutters.

She nods, turning to glance at the building and then back to me. "Yep. This is me. Home sweet home. Davis... look, I know this is crazy, but... I'm not ready for tonight to be over," she says. "I mean... today? Whatever."

The sun's rising, and it's got to be after six, and I

should be exhausted after being awake for almost twenty-four hours, but I'm not tired. If anything, I'm on a high after tonight, a combination of adrenaline and want for the fiery, beautiful girl standing in front of me making my heart race.

"Who says it has to?"

She laughs. "Uh… the sun coming up?"

"Always the smart-ass," I chuckle as I step forward, curve my palm over her hip, and pull her against me, closing the distance between us. "Doesn't mean it has to be over. I dunno, maybe it's just beginning."

"Oh?" Her brow arches.

"Let me take you out again. Today? Brunch?"

I want her to say yes, even more than I want to kiss her right now, and that's pretty fucking bad.

I want to spend the rest of the day kissing her, showing her just how badly I want her after getting on my knees for her.

It went too fucking quick, and I want more.

Her eyes search mine, a beat of silence hanging between us, and then a sexy, teasing grin flits to her lips, and she steps back, letting go of my shirt as she starts to step backward toward her house. "Mmmm, I dunno, Loverboy. The auction rules say I only have you for a single night, remember?"

The closer she gets to the house, the harder my heart races. There's no way she's walking through that door without me finding a way to talk to her again.

Her number.

Her socials.

Her fucking student email.

Something.

"Well, we both know how much fun breaking the rules is. C'mon, Trouble, give me *something*," I murmur, giving her my best smile. "Break the rules with me."

Pulling her plump lip between her teeth, she rolls her eyes, biting back a smirk. "Three eight six, fourteen eleven. How about if you can convince me to break the rules... I just might." She turns on her heel toward the town house, disappearing through the front door without a backward glance.

I quickly pull my phone from my pocket and input the number she rattled off.

She wants me to chase her? Convince her to keep seeing me?

Well, there's only one thing I'm better at than baseball.

Persuasion.

chapter seven

Zara

"Obsessed"— Zandros, Limi

Loverboy: I can't stop thinking about how sweet your pussy tasted.

Loverboy: I need to see you again before I lose my fucking mind. C'mon, Trouble, put me out of my misery.

Trouble: Sorry working on an essay right now. Reallllllllly busy. Maybe soon...😇😈

> Loverboy: You know what's better than writing a philosophy essay?
>
> Trouble: Not writing a philosophy essay...?
>
> Loverboy: Nah, writing it with me there... 😈
>
> PICTURE ATTACHMENT

Oh. My. God.

It's been two days of messages just like this, and admittedly, my resolve to play hard to get is lessening by the second.

Not that there was very much to begin with.

Davis Guidry is *impossible* to resist.

Something I should've known the moment I decided to play this little *game* with him because now he's not the only one who's suffering.

Trust me, misery loves company.

The picture on my screen is enough to set my skin on fire and my clit throbbing in cadence with my pounding heart.

He's so ridiculously fucking hot that he's single-handedly bringing *back* mirror pictures.

In the photo, the mirror is slightly fogged from his shower, and he's standing there in nothing but a white towel that's knotted at the front, hanging low on his hips and giving just enough of a view to make me want

Rookie Mistake

to lick every drop of water cascading down those delicious, chiseled abs. The sight of the tattoo on his hip makes me shiver, unable to stop myself from thinking about the night we spent together.

"Is that your *Loverboy* again?" Harper asks from beside me, causing me to jump. "He's not even trying to hide how down bad he is for you. He's double texting. The definition of a man obsessed."

Laughing haughtily, I toss my phone onto the bed, dragging my attention back to my computer, where I'm supposed to be writing said essay for philosophy.

"He's... *fun*."

Lily hums from her spot at the foot of the bed, shooting me a look with a raised brow.

God, it's like they know me or something.

I mean... only better than anyone else on the planet, but still.

They know that fun is my thing, and that's exactly why I love this thing between Davis and me. It's *fun* with no pressure or expectations. We're both free to do whatever it is we please, and it just so happens that right now, we both want to do each other.

Harper swipes my phone off the bed and punches in my passcode to unlock it, gazing down at the screen. Her eyes widen when she reads the latest text, followed by the photo he sent. "Zara, my god. The man is nearly begging to eat you like his last meal. Those abs? You're insane. Let him come over. I'm texting him back. *Right. Now.*" Before I can even reach for my phone, her fingers fly across the screen, and then she glances up at me with a shit-eating smirk. "There."

She turns my phone to face me, and my eyes scan the message she replied with.

Trouble: Well since you asked so nicely like a good boy... How about right now?

"Harper!" I shriek, slamming my laptop shut and pushing it to the side. "You can't just invite him over right now. I have... homework, and I haven't even shaved my legs today."

I realize, even as I say it, how ridiculous those excuses sound because we all know the last thing I'm worried about right now is homework, and if a man is put off by a little hair on my legs, then clearly, he's not a man.

I'm just making excuses.

Mostly because as badly as I want Davis, I'm also the tiniest bit afraid of the way I feel when I'm with him. How much I like just being *with* him. How easy it feels.

Because the last thing I want or need is to get involved with any guy at OU besides a casual, *fun* hookup.

There, that's the cold, hard truth. Something I haven't even admitted out loud to my best friends.

"Oh shit, he's responding, he's responding!" Harper says, bouncing on the bed with my phone in hand once more. Even Lily looks interested, and that's something I wasn't expecting.

"This is an absolutely terrible idea. What happens if Oliver comes home and finds some random guy here? He's going to go ballistic," I say.

Harper rolls her eyes. "First of all, Oliver needs to chill the fuck out. He's not your father. Despite what he likes to think, you're a whole-ass adult. He can't treat you like you're a child your whole life, Zara. Plus, isn't he at his flavor of the week's for the night? Hypocrite."

"Yes, bu—"

She lifts a hand, "Nope. No buts. Look, you made a promise to yourself that you'd have the best year of your life, and clearly, this man is the fun you need. Honestly... I'm surprised I'm even having to talk you into this right now. You're usually the one to jump at a new hookup."

I'm quiet for a moment, chewing my lip while I think about my options. Finally, I sigh. "I'm just... I don't want to get attached, and Davis is the kind of guy that would make it easy to."

Harper's face softens, and she nods, understanding shining in her eyes. "I get it, babe, I do. But I think that if you're interested in him and you want to have fun, then just have that conversation. Friends with benefits. Simple, no strings attached. Communication is everything."

Without a doubt, this is what I want. I just want to

make sure that I keep my freshman year fun and drama-free.

Hooking up with the same guy on the regular sometimes makes that not very easy.

"You're right. What did he say?"

Her eyes light up before dropping back to the screen. *"See you soon, Trouble."*

WHEN HE SHOWS up an hour later, thankfully after I kicked Harper and Lily out the door, I'm… nervous. For the first time in a very long time.

Like I'm going on a first date or meeting someone for the first time and not like I haven't already had one of the best sexual experiences of my life with the guy.

It's a foreign feeling, one that I'm not accustomed to, that has my stomach flipping as I swing the front door open and see him standing on the other side wearing a cocky, dimpled grin.

It's only been two days since I've seen him, and somehow, it's like I've forgotten how hot he is until now that he's standing here in front of me.

It doesn't at all help the fluttering in my stomach or the wild thrash of my heart.

Unlike the night of the auction, tonight, he's dressed

casually in black athletic shorts and a worn gray cutoff shirt that shows the tanned, sculpted muscles along his sides, along with an old baseball hat.

"Hi," he murmurs.

"Hi."

His smirk widens, and I step back, holding the door open, allowing him to step inside. When he passes, brushing against me, the scent of his bodywash, fresh and clean, invades my nostrils and makes my core clench.

Shutting the door, I turn to face him, watching as he looks around my living room. I've only lived here since the summer, but I've been trying to make it less like a bachelor pad a little at a time.

"I like your house."

I cross my arms over my chest and smirk, popping a brow. "Did you come over for small talk or..."

"*Brat.*" He chuckles.

I force my gaze from his and bite back a smile.

Surprisingly, my favorite part about Davis *isn't* how talented he is with his tongue but how much fun it is to talk shit to him and the fact that he never hesitates to talk shit right back.

It may be my favorite version of foreplay.

He walks over to me in long, measured strides and stops in front of me, reaching up to finger the end of my wet hair, rolling the strands between two fingers. "You know exactly why I'm here, Zara."

I swallow roughly, sucking in a breath as I try not to clench my thighs together at the low, raspy baritone that's full of promise.

"Mmm, do I?"

My words are breathless, betraying exactly how I'm feeling right now, and he smirks, dropping the strand of my hair that he was twirling around his finger. "I haven't been able to stop thinking about you, and something tells me you haven't been able to stop thinking about me either."

"I thought this was supposed to be one night."

"Yeah, well, one night wasn't enough. In fact, I barely got a taste. Wasn't nearly enough," he responds, licking his lips as his gaze drops to mine. "I love these painted red, but fuck, they're even prettier when they're not. Gimme another taste, Zara."

When he lifts his hand and sweeps his thumb across my lip, a shiver racks my spine, and my nipples tighten into hardened peaks that press against the fabric of my cotton tank. The friction is deliciously torturous.

I want him.

We have this insane... tangible chemistry that I couldn't deny even if I tried.

It's palpable, a magnetic field of tension that is terrifyingly powerful.

And right now, I want to climb on top of him and chase that feeling, but I also know that this can't keep happening unless we lay down some type of boundaries.

I don't want to be in my head about this, and clear expectations make things easy.

My specialty.

"If we do this again, it's just for fun. I told you at the bar that I'm not looking for anything complicated, and that still stands," I say.

His thick brow lifts. "I know. I remember your commitment phobia."

The teasing tone of his voice has me shaking my head as I place my hand on his shoulder and push it playfully. "I'm serious. That's the only way. If you want to hook up and have fun, then I'm down, but that's all it'll be."

There's a beat of silence between us as his amber eyes hold mine intently, and then he shrugs. "If that's what you want, then I'm good with it. But I should warn you, I'm extremely lovable. *You* might be the one to fall in love with *me*, Trouble."

My scoff echoes around the living room, and his smirk widens, offering me another dip of his shoulder. "Trust me, that's not going to be a problem," I tell him, stepping closer until my still-pebbled nipples brush against the front of his T-shirt. I rise on my tiptoes and weave my fingers into the hair at his nape.

His breath hitches slightly, and I can see pools of heat flaring in his eyes.

"Now that we know exactly what this is, how about we stop talking?" I slide my hand along his stomach, his muscles contracting beneath my fingers, trailing lower until I reach the waistband of his shorts. "There's something I need to do."

"Yeah?"

I nod, raking my teeth over my bottom lip as I peer up at him through my lashes. He slides his arm around my waist and tugs me against him. The path his fingers trace along my back has a flurry of goose bumps erupting along my flesh.

"Something I've been thinking about since the night of the auction."

His mouth falls open in surprise when I drop to my knees in front of him, tilting my head back to gaze back at him.

Our eyes lock.

Lifting my hand, I curve my palm over his already hardening cock through his shorts, pulling a low groan from him. My fingers wrap around his length, and I squeeze, never taking my eyes off his.

The intensity of our eye contact alone is enough to have my thighs rubbing together, chasing friction and a pent-up release.

"And I can't wait another second," I murmur, tugging the fabric of his shorts and briefs while he gazes down at me with heated eyes.

I've never felt sexier in my life than I do right now,

on my knees for him, simply by the way he's looking at me.

Using both hands, I pull his shorts and briefs all the way down, freeing his cock. It bobs between us, impossibly thick and long. The head is dark red and angry, seeping a pearly bead of precum from the slit that I can't wait to catch on my tongue.

I bring my fist to his velvety erection and circle it, my eyes widening when my fingers don't meet.

God, he's huge. Completely proportionate with his body. Yet, I'm still shocked by the size.

"You're doing great things for my ego staring at my cock like that," he rasps, dragging a thumb across my bottom lip.

He has no idea just how badly I've wanted to do this since he got on his knees for me in the back room of that bar. This is just as much for *me* as it is for him.

Using both hands to fist the base of his cock, I guide him to my mouth and swipe my tongue at the precum that's coating the ridge of this thick head.

After licking him clean, I drag my tongue down the length of the vein before closing my lips around the head and taking him deeper into my mouth, inch by inch.

I keep my gaze trained on him because god, he looks so fucking hot right now.

I can't stop watching him.

His head drops back on his shoulders, his throat

bobbing as a low, guttural groan vibrates from his chest. His fingers sink into my hair, completely lost in the feel of my mouth on him.

"Fuuuuuck, Zara."

Each syllable makes my core throb and my clit pulse wildly.

I take him deeper into my mouth, cupping his heavy balls, rolling them in my hands. His hips flex reflexively, pushing his cock to the back of my throat, and I take it eagerly.

"Goddamnit. Why are you so fucking perfect? A fucking goddess on your knees." I think I've developed a praise kink when it comes to him, or maybe it's been here all along and he's the one who's brought it to the surface because heat floods my belly, and I swear that I could come just by sucking his cock.

Suddenly, he's pulling me off him, his chest heaving with the motion as he tugs me to my feet. "Fuck this. I want you to soak my face while I fuck your throat." With that, he bends and throws me over his shoulder. "Where's your bedroom, Trouble?"

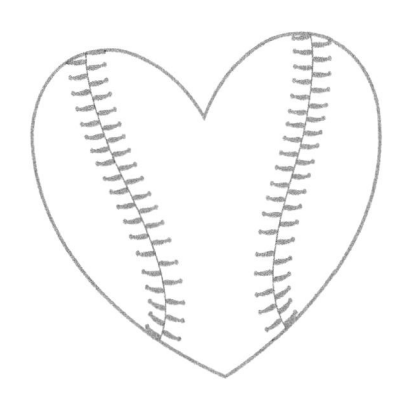

chapter eight
Davis

"Into it"— Chase Atlantic

I don't even stop to look around her room. I toss her onto the mattress, where she scrambles for me, throwing her arms around my neck and slamming her lips on mine.

We're both frantic, needy. A clash of teeth and hands that I can hardly keep track of.

Her tongue sweeps through the seam of my lips, dancing with mine, and I can still taste me lingering.

I can't fucking get enough of her.

Every piece she gives me, it only makes me desperate for more, a high that I want to chase over and over.

She rips at my shirt, trying to pull it over my head, so I tear my lips from hers and reach behind my neck, pulling it off and tossing it aside.

I watch as she grasps at the hem of her tank and drags it off. She's naked beneath it, and my gaze drops to her tits.

The perfect fucking handfuls. Heavy and full. So fucking sexy.

Her nipples are the prettiest dusty pink, tightened into pebbled peaks.

And there's a trail of dark black ink that runs between the valley of her tits along pale, creamy skin.

A combination of notes and bar lines and various musical symbols.

She's the hottest thing I've ever seen, and just looking at her perfect body makes me so goddamn hard that I can't help but palm my cock, pumping it once as I take her in.

Her eyes darken as she watches me fuck my fist.

"That make you wet, baby?"

She nods, sucking on that plump lip.

"Show me," I rasp.

Dropping back onto the bed, she sits up on her elbows and spreads her legs, shimmying out of her shorts and panties, leaving her completely bare for my eyes.

When she uses her fingers to spread her pussy open, giving me exactly what I asked for, I feel my balls tightening as arousal tugs at the base of my spine.

She's so fucking sexy I don't know how I'm going to last before I even get inside her. I already came today thinking about her, imagining what she'd look like in this moment, and fuck, it pales in comparison.

"Good girl. Now, rub your clit for me. Slow circles." I grip the base of my cock and squeeze.

My dick is throbbing at the sight of her spread out, her pretty pink little pussy wet and glistening in the pale lamplight. She's so wet it's trickling down her, dripping onto her tight little hole that I want to fuck with my tongue and then my cock one day.

I thought I could play this game with her, let her fuck herself while I watched, but I can't wait to touch her. Taste her cunt again.

I crawl onto the mattress and lift her foot, pressing my lips along the inside of her ankle, crafting a trail up her calf, dragging my tongue along the back of her knee, the inside of her thigh. Tasting every inch of her skin.

"I can't decide what I want more. Should I fuck your throat while I eat your cunt, or should you ride my face until you're dripping down my chin?"

Zara stares up at me, those pretty green eyes blazing. "Both."

I grin.

That's my good girl.

I flop down onto the mattress next to her and tug her on top of me. "Then get up here and give me a taste."

She doesn't hesitate for even a second, climbing over my face and positioning that sweet little pussy right where I want it. With her thighs on each side of my head, I can feel her wet heat as her pussy hovers over my mouth.

Fuck, I love the way she tastes.

Her palms rest on my thighs as she finally lowers herself to my mouth, and I close my lips around her clit and suck hard, tugging it into my mouth and rolling it between my lips until her hips rock, adding to the motion of my tongue.

"Oh god," she cries, arching her back. "God, you feel so good."

She has no fucking idea. I could die right here, drowning on her pussy, and I still wouldn't have enough of it.

My dick is practically weeping right now as she takes me in her mouth, immediately sliding me down her throat until she's gagging.

I groan against her pussy, the vibrations making her whimper, and then I curve my palms over her hips, guiding her back and forth on my mouth.

When she moans around my cock, I almost fucking come. My balls are aching for release, and I want to bury myself in her throat and fill it with every drop of me.

It doesn't take long for her to come, riding my face. She rocks her hips in needy, frantic motions as she pants, licking at my cock like it's a fucking lollipop.

The moment she comes, her entire body seizes, her thighs tremble, and she floods my mouth, giving me the sweetest taste of my fucking life.

I lap it all up, flattening my tongue and drinking every drop down.

After the orgasm rocks through her and I wring every ounce of pleasure out of her that I can, she collapses on top of me, her cheek pressed against my thigh.

Her body heaves, chest rising and falling as she tries to return her breathing to normal.

Sliding my hands up her body, I pick her up and flip her until she's sprawled along my chest, ear pressed to the erratic beat of my heart.

The rough pads of my fingers dance along her spine lazily, neither of us moving.

"I think I'm obsessed with your dick," she pants, hands on my chest as she rises to look at me.

I lift from the bed and suck her nipple into my mouth, grazing my teeth over the sensitive peak. Her back arches, her fingers flying to my hair, holding me against her sensitive skin.

"It's a great dick to be obsessed with."

I take my time with each nipple, giving each attention before she tugs at my hair, causing me to lift my eyes to her.

"Stop talking and *fuck me*," she pants, reaching between us and wrapping her soft hand around my cock, squeezing until a pearl of precum beads at the slit. Her pink tongue darts out, and she licks her lips, as if there's nothing more she wants than to taste my cum.

Dirty girl.

And so fucking hot. I love that she doesn't hold back. She says exactly what she's thinking and isn't afraid to ask for what she wants.

"You need me to fuck you?"

I reach up, cupping her pert tit in my palm, ghosting my thumb over her nipple before tweaking it between my fingers roughly, rolling and tugging.

She tosses her head back on her shoulders, that wave of long, inky-black hair tickling the tops of my thighs as she rocks her hips and grinds her pussy along my thighs.

"Yes. *Please*." Her nails bite into my chest as she flexes them with each word. "Or… I'll just have to take care of it myself."

She's provoking me, and fuck, it's working.

I grab the soft flare of her hips with both palms, dragging her forward until she's settled directly over my cock.

Zara groans wickedly as she bites her bottom lip,

Rookie Mistake

gazing down at me through her thick, dark lashes, and rocks her hips, coating me with her arousal. Now I know not only how good she tastes but how hot and wet her cunt feels on my bare cock. Soft and velvet, I groan out loud at the contact. She feels like fucking pure bliss, and I want to sink inside of her, over and over, until we've both had our fill.

I could watch her all fucking night, just like this, and still not have enough.

She could easily become an addiction if I'm not careful. This girl has something that I know I could get lost in.

"How about *you* fuck *me*?" I rasp, using my hands on her hips, rolling her over my cock again. This time, her clit drags against the thick head, and she gasps, her eyes fluttering closed while her fingers embed themselves in my chest, leaving behind a delicious bite of pain and crescent-moon-shaped imprints that I'll wear like a goddamn medal. "Ride my cock, Trouble."

Her lips fall open each time her hips rock, and my dick juts against her swollen clit over and over again, a breathy, hot-as-fuck whimper tumbles from her.

Reaching between us, she wraps her hand around my length, guiding me to her entrance, and she slowly sinks down an inch, putting only the head of my cock inside her.

We groan in unison, the sound filling the air between us as my fingers tighten on her hips. It feels so fucking good I have to fight to keep my eyes open so I can watch her. I want to see her face when she sinks all the way down and has my cock buried deep inside her cunt. I want to watch me fill her pussy and watch her bounce on my dick, those pretty tits swaying. I don't just want it... I *need* it.

"God, I don't... It's not going to fit. You're too big," she whines breathlessly as she starts to work a little more inside of her.

I lift the rough pad of my thumb to her clit and draw slow, lazy circles until her lips part and her head falls back on her shoulders, slowly relaxing.

"Don't worry, baby. We'll loosen that pussy up, get you ready to take every inch of me." My voice is hoarse as I fight for control, the overwhelming need to come trickling down my spine. I've never had an issue with stamina, but tonight, my restraint is threadbare.

Nearly nonexistent.

She has me so fucking wound up right now that I might come before I even get all the way inside of her.

The longer I strum her clit, increasing the pressure with each sweep of my thumb, the more she relaxes, sinking down tortuously slowly until my cock is buried to the hilt.

I feel like I'm going to lose my mind from the feel of her wet heat wrapped around my dick. It's indescribable.

My palms drag up her hips to her rib cage, where I

cup her tits in each hand, sweeping my thumb over her pebbled nipples.

Admiring every inch of the masterpiece she is.

The sound of her shaky exhale echoes around the room as she tries to adjust to my size.

When I roll her taut nipple between my thumb and finger, she hums a low sound of approval. Her palms flatten along my chest as she lifts her hips, sliding off my cock until only the tip remains inside of her, then slams back down, impaling herself roughly.

Holy fuck.

The corners of my vision dim as she begins to ride me, lifting on her knees to bounce on my cock, taking her pleasure unabashedly.

Every muscle in my body coils tight when she bottoms out, my cock sinking so far inside of her that it reaches resistance. Her swollen clit brushes against the short hair of my groin as she finds her rhythm, creating delicious friction that has us both panting.

She's already close. I can feel her walls beginning to tighten around me, but I'm nowhere near done with her. I'm going to fuck Zara so good and make her come so hard she's not going to be able to walk tomorrow without feeling the reminder of what I felt like buried in her guts.

A deep groan vibrates from my chest when she rotates her hips, and my cock brushes against her G-spot.

"Right there, oh god. *Davis.*"

My name sounds like a forbidden prayer, and it makes me even harder. I lift my hips to slam into her, thrusting up to meet her every time she drops back down. My balls draw up as I feel her pussy clench around me as she comes, her cunt squeezing my dick like a vise. She falls forward onto my chest, trembling with each wave of her orgasm, breathlessly chanting my name over and over, her pussy still fluttering around my dick.

It's fucking *magnificent* to witness.

It takes all the control I possess not to follow behind her when my balls are aching to spill inside of her, but I'm not done.

I'm dragging this out as long as I can.

She's still coming as I flip us in one smooth motion, placing her back flat on the bed as I put her leg on my shoulder and thrust back inside of her. Her pussy contracts with the aftershocks of her orgasm as I fuck her, my hips slamming against the back of her thighs.

The sound is like a symphony as it fills the room, an erotic mixture of our breathing and the sound of our skin meeting.

I dip my head to her nipple as I palm her breast, lifting it to my lips and sucking it into my mouth, letting my teeth graze the tip, pulling a whimper from Zara.

I rotate my hips, swiveling my cock inside her, and watch as her eyes flutter shut, those dark lashes fanning against her cheeks. Lifting off her slightly, I can peer down between us to watch my cock sliding in and out of her. Her pretty little cunt is pink and glistening from her orgasm, her creamy arousal coating my cock as it disappears into her.

"I wish you could see how pretty your pussy looks right now, stretching to take my cock. Fuck, I can't wait to see my cum dripping out of you. I want you to push it out so I can watch it drip to your tight little asshole." I lightly slap her clit, and she moans so loud I do it again and again until she's writhing beneath me. "I want to cover you in my cum. Your pussy, your ass, your mouth. Paint your creamy tits with it."

My filthy words seem to unlock something inside her. Her eyes snap open, and she curves her palm at my nape, yanking me toward her and slamming her lips on mine. She moans into my mouth as my tongue dances with hers, both of us frantic as my hips rock slow and deep, hitting that part inside of her with each thrust that has her clamping down around my cock again.

Her nails claw at my back when I increase my pace, fucking her into the mattress. My spine tingles, my balls drawing tight, ready for release, when I pull out of her abruptly, my chest heaving as I sit back, heel to thigh.

"On your knees, baby. Ass up."

She doesn't hesitate, flipping onto her stomach and putting her ass in the air, shimming her hips back and forth.

How the fuck is she even sexier like this? Face pressed into the mattress, her dripping pussy opened to me and heart-shaped ass right in my face, ready for me to devour or fuck or *both*.

I rise to my knees behind her and grip her ass, spreading her cheeks so I can look at her.

Groaning, I shake my head. "You're so fucking perfect, Zara. You have no idea all the things I want to do to you."

She looks back at me over her shoulder, breathing heavily and her cheeks flushed. "Next time. Please put your dick back inside of me before I die."

Because I promised to be a good boy, I listen, slamming back inside of her while I grip her ass. We both groan as I begin to fuck her from behind, each of my thrusts hard and deep as if I'm trying to mold myself inside of her. My balls slap her clit, and it feels so goddamn good my eyes nearly roll back.

I'm not going to last much longer, not when she's got a magical fucking pussy that makes me lose my damn head.

The tips of my fingers dig into her ass to spread her open wider, and I bring the tip of my thumb to the tight ring of her ass and press lightly.

She hisses, her back arching as I circle it, pressing inside slightly.

"Are you going to come like my good girl if I stick my finger in your tight little ass, Trouble?" I don't push any further, wanting to hear her consent. I watch as she nods frantically against the mattress. "Tell me you want me to finger your ass, and I'll give it to you."

"I want you to fuck my ass, Davis," she murmurs. She pushes back against my finger, and it's all I need to go further.

I spit on the tight ring, using my thumb to spread the wetness around, coating her before I push the full tip of my finger inside.

"Oh my god." Her voice is low and hoarse, full of need.

I hum a groan in response, the small amount of restraint I had left fraying at the edges and snapping. I slide my thumb into her slowly until it's buried in her tight ass while my cock is balls-deep in her pussy.

So fucking full of me.

Her hips push back to meet my thrusts, and every time I slip my thumb out of her ass, I slam my hips back inside of her, thrusting so hard I'm fucking her up on the bed. Her head's nearly hitting the headboard.

"Coming, coming, coming," she pants as her knuckles turn white from fisting the sheets. "Fuck, I'm coming."

Her pussy clamps down on my cock as I follow her over the edge of oblivion. I thrust deep, rutting against her cervix as I explode, emptying inside of her.

Just as I promised, I fill her with my cum, my thrusts

slowing languidly as she milks my cock with her tight heat, greedily taking every drop.

A surge of possessiveness surges through me when I pull out of her, watching a small trail of my cum trickle out of her, down to her swollen clit.

I spread her open, admiring the sight. "Push it out, baby. Let me see my cum dripping out of the pussy I just fucked."

She whimpers, and I watch as she squeezes her inner walls, contracting to push my cum out. It oozes out of her cunt, and I swear my dick nearly gets hard again.

"Good girl," I praise, scooping my cum with two fingers and shoving it back deep inside of her. I press my lips to her clit in a quick kiss before I rise from the bed and head to the bathroom for a warm washcloth.

When I return, she's lying on her side, cuddling into the covers with her eyes dropped shut.

"Sleepy," she mumbles while I part her thighs and drag the warm cloth over her, cleaning her. Sex has always been good. Great, even, with the right girl.

But *this*?

This is something entirely different. This is fucking cosmic. Indescribable.

Not that I've ever been good with words, but they fail me right now.

This girl is going to bring me to my knees. Again. And I'd gladly stay there if it meant I could taste her cunt again.

This was the best sex of my life.

I flop down onto the mattress next to her and gather her into my arms, both of us taking a second to catch our breath.

"Oh fuck," Zara whispers a while later. I've almost drifted off when her body suddenly goes tense against me. *"Shit, shit, shit."*

A car door shuts outside, and her emerald eyes widen. She looks so goddamn pretty right now, her hair mussed from my fingers, her lips still swollen and pink from my mouth that I honestly am having a hard time focusing on anything else.

Can you blame me?

Suddenly, she scrambles away from me and out of the bed before I can even ask what the fuck's happening. She starts searching blindly for her discarded clothes, and when she sees I'm still lying there with my dick out, she halts.

"You have to go. *Now.*"

Then my T-shirt comes flying toward me, nailing me in the face. I pull it off, staring over at her in confusion. "What? Why? Give me like ten minutes, and I'm good to go again."

She pulls the tank over her head and starts to pull up her panties, shaking her head. "No, you don't understand. My brother has apparently decided to come home tonight, even though he wasn't supposed to be coming home, and he cannot find you here. He'll never let me out of the house again. Davis, seriously, get dressed!"

I haven't even been able to bask in the glow of the mind-blowing sex we just had, and she's already kicking me out.

Damn.

Rising from the bed, I hurriedly tug my T-shirt over my head, then grab my briefs from the floor and slide them on.

"You're not allowed to have people over?"

"Not guys. My brother is… stupid and overprotective. He'll lose his mind if he catches you here, and I do not feel like dealing with his shit tonight," she says as she walks over to the window and peers out of it. "You're gonna have to go out the window."

"Be for real," I laugh.

When I see her expression, that it's dead serious, my eyes widen. "You want me to sneak out of your window?"

She nods, chewing on the corner of her lip and scrunching her nose. "Yeah, sorry."

Smirking, I shrug. "Well, this is a first. I actually haven't ever snuck out of someone's window before."

I quickly pull her to me and press my lips to hers, stealing a kiss because if I'm crawling out of a goddamn window like we're in high school again, I've gotta taste those lips one more time.

She giggles against my mouth as she pushes at my

chest, pulling away. "Stop it. Pants. You have to find your pa—" There's a noise outside of her bedroom door, and she freezes, cursing quietly. "Shit."

"Zara, who's in your room?" a deep voice comes from the other side of the door.

There's a pause, and she sighs, shaking her head. "No one. Go away."

"Fuck that. I'm not going away," the voice replies just as I find my pants next to her desk. The door flies open, and I'm standing there like a deer in fucking headlights in nothing but my briefs, covering my dick with my balled-up shorts.

Of course, the first time we hook up, we get busted by her brother, *pantless*.

Because that's just my fucking luck.

Two things happen at once.

All in slow motion, or at least that's what it feels like.

1. Zara loses her shit.

And… 2. I realize that her brother?

Oliver fucking Andrews, enemy number one and the guy vying for my spot as starting pitcher.

We *hate* each other, and I just had sex with his sister. In his house.

Mother. Fucker.

chapter nine

Zara

"Dangerously"— Charlie Puth

If you thought there was *anything* worse than your older brother walking in on you and the guy you just had sex with who turns out has the biggest dick you've *ever* seen and fucks like a god but coincidentally is said brother's number one rival... you'd be wrong.

Trust me, I'd know.

And just when I thought the situation couldn't have gone from bad to worse, it *absolutely* did.

It went from being incredible to being a total shitshow.

I had to physically push Oliver out of my bedroom when he started acting like a complete and utter overbearing asshole. But that wasn't the surprising part.

Obviously, I knew that Davis was a baseball player, but what I *didn't* know is that he and Oliver *hate* each other, and their rivalry is a huge issue for the baseball team, causing tensions to run extremely high.

"You're *not* seeing him again, Zara. I... I forbid it," Oliver barks, rubbing his palm over his jaw at the kitchen island the following morning. "That guy is a fucking asshole and a total womanizer, and I don't want you around him."

I'm running on very little sleep, and honestly, even if I'd had a full eight hours, I still wouldn't want to be dealing with yet another conversation with my brother, who clearly is delusional.

God, is this what my entire four years of college is going to be like? Oliver acting like I'm a petulant child and not respecting any of the boundaries I've set?

"Funny that *he's* the asshole when you're the one who acted like a complete dick, yet he was perfectly polite to you despite that. And I'm just going to pretend you didn't just say that 'forbid' comment because you've clearly lost your mind. I'm a grown-ass woman, Oliver. You aren't protecting me—you're smothering me. You're not respecting my boundaries, which I am clearly laying down for you. You're trying to control every aspect of my life, and it's not happening."

His mouth parts in surprise and then snaps shut.

My brow arches.

I never lie down and take his bullshit, but this... this is different. Last night was the last straw.

"You're going to stop dictating my life. Who I'm with, where I'm going. What I wear. It's completely unacceptable and disrespectful that you know I feel this way and you continue to do these things, and then you report back to Dad like you're my handler."

"Look, sure, I might have been a dick last night, but I just walked in on my little sister... doing things I don't even want to think about with a guy I can't fucking stand," he spits, face full of fury, blazing in his eyes.

Hopping down from the barstool, I shake my head, stopping him. "Oliver, I love you. You're my big brother. But stop. Seriously. I don't want to fight with you, but I'm an adult, and I'm going to make my own choices, my own decisions, and my own opinions. I understand that you and Davis have... issues. But that's between you. If I decide to stop seeing him, it's going to be because I wanted to, not because it had anything to do with you. Got it?"

For the first time in his life, my brother's speechless, and I'm feeling much, much better now that I've gotten that off my chest.

Growing up, we were always close. Oliver's only

one year older than me, and I was always his little shadow. Wherever he went, I went, and people often mistook us as twins because of our dark hair and matching green eyes. Our parents were always busy with my father's business, and he was always my big brother who took care of me.

But as much as I love him and as close as we've always been, it doesn't give him the right to dictate my life or be an asshole to those I care about.

Does Davis fall under that category?

I reach past him to grab a banana out of the fruit bowl and offer a wide smile. "Nice talk. Gotta run, I'm going to be late for class."

I don't even bother to wait for his response because even if he was going to try and fight with me, it wouldn't matter. I said exactly what needed to be said. What I honestly probably should've already said way before now. Like the time he took out a ruler and measured my skirt like a total psycho.

I texted Davis this morning with the hopes of apologizing, and he agreed to meet me in the quad so we could talk after my musical theory class. I find him sitting on a bench outside of the fine arts building when I walk out of the doors.

He looks absolutely delicious, to absolutely no surprise, wearing a pair of faded jeans with a red OU T-shirt and that backward baseball hat that I'm quickly realizing how much I like.

I love seeing him without a hat and running my fingers through his hair, especially when he's between my thighs, but I love him in the hat almost as much. The ends of his hair curl from beneath it, and when he glances up, a dimpled smile overtakes his face as if he's happy to see me.

"Hi," I breathe as I sink down onto the bench and set my backpack beside me, turning to face him.

Being this close to him, being surrounded by the fresh, woodsy scent of him, already has my senses on overdrive. It's impossible not to think about the last time we were together and how much I want it to happen again.

And again. And again.

"How's your day?" he asks.

I laugh with a shake of my head, tucking a strand of hair behind my ear. "I'm tired, and I basically told my brother to fuck off and to stop trying to control my life over breakfast this morning. But you know, other than that, it's been great. I texted you to meet me here because I wanted to apologize for the way he acted. So embarrassing, honestly."

"You don't have to apologize for him, Zara. Shit with us is... tense, but it doesn't have anything to do with you," he says.

I nod. "Yeah, but I just didn't like how it went down, and that's kind of what I wanted to talk to you about. My brother doesn't make decisions for me." I pause, rolling my lips together. "And truthfully? Hanging out with you has been really fun, and if you wanted to continue to see each other, then I'm down. This thing with the two of you is between you two, not between us."

His lip tilts as he lifts a brow and leans closer. "I'm down. Fuck yeah, I'm down."

"And like we said, we keep it casual. No strings attached. *Fun.*"

"I love fun," he breathes cheekily.

Laughing, I run my fingers along the edge of my leather miniskirt before dragging my gaze back to his. "But I do think we should keep it on the DL? Even though I'm staying out of this whole thing between you two, he's my brother, and as stupid as he can be at times, I love him, and I don't want to make things worse. It would probably make it even more difficult when the season starts. So, I figure it's easier if he doesn't really know we're still hanging out."

Davis nods, his warm honey eyes softening. "I get it. No more fun at your house. You can always come to my apartment. It's not as clean and definitely doesn't smell as good, seeing as how I live with a bunch of sweaty assholes, but you don't have to worry about sneaking out of any windows."

"God, you're never going to let that go, are you?"

"Nope." He grins, reaching for my hand, and threads his fingers in mine. The pad of his thumb sweeps over the tattoos on my fingers, something he seems to like to do since he's done it so much since the night we met. "I've got to get to class, and I've got a pitching session right after, but come over later? Honestly, I can't cook for shit, but I can order Jack's? Maybe we can watch Netflix or something."

"Jesus, Loverboy, did you just try to Netflix and chill me?"

A laugh rumbles from his chest. "God, you're such a fucking brat." A beat passes, and he leans in, ghosting his lips along mine, inhaling. "Tell me why I like it so much?"

"Because you like trouble."

"Mhmm," he hums. "Seems like I've got a thing for it. I think I told you what I was going to do to see if you'd still be a brat. I'll see you tonight. Wear the lipstick, Trouble."

Shit.

I clench my thighs together as he presses a hot, lingering kiss against my lips and then rises to his feet. He picks up his backpack off the sidewalk, shoots me a wink, then strides off, leaving my heart racing and anticipation surging through my body.

DAVIS'S APARTMENT is just outside of fraternity row, in a building that's original to campus. Obviously, it's older, but it has a certain charm that a lot of the new construction places lack.

It's cute, and quaint, and not at all what you would expect a group of college athletes to live in, but I'm pleasantly surprised by how clean and tidy everything is.

"I like your house," I tease, repeating his words back to him from the night at my house.

When he doesn't respond, I drag my attention to where he's standing, leaned against the doorframe, his gaze hungrily running down my body in an unhurried perusal.

"Fuck, Trouble, you can't come over here wearing that," he murmurs, crossing the distance between us in a few steps. "I don't wanna have to fight my roommates."

I laugh and shake my head with an eye roll.

I'm not wearing anything special, just an old pair of shorts that used to be baggy jeans until I cut them up and a black babydoll crop top with an old pair of Nikes.

Definitely not as sexy as the night we met, but I guess he likes me dressed down just as much.

"No fighting."

He smirks, dipping his shoulder. "No promises." Sliding an arm around my waist, he pulls me to him and hugs me.

A lingering hug that feels far more intimate than it should.

I clear my throat and step back. "So, where are these roommates?"

"A party, I think? Who knows, honestly."

"And you didn't feel like a party tonight? Parties are... fun."

Another shrug. "I try not to go out on a weeknight because my schedule is always so packed, and it's hard to juggle it all. Plus... last year, I got into a bit of trouble. Drinking too much, people posting pictures on social media. My coach had my ass, so I'm trying to stay straight this year."

Now, this, I can see. Davis seems to be the kind of guy who walks into a room and commands attention. He's the life of a party. The charming, infectious guy. And I can absolutely see why he's got the playboy reputation.

"Ah, but trouble seems to find you, clearly."

Laughing, he drags a hand over his jaw and nods. "Obviously, so that's why you're here. But, you know." He steps closer, sliding a palm over my hip and tugging me closer. "I think you're the kinda trouble that's worth it."

"Glad to hear it, Loverboy." I lift on my tiptoes and give him a quick kiss before stepping back and walking around his apartment, taking it all in.

It's clean and pretty basic, but at the same time, it

feels like a home and not a party place, which is pretty common for college housing.

"I was going to order takeout tonight, but I had a better idea. You up for going somewhere instead?"

"Sure."

An hour later, we're sitting on his tailgate in the parking lot of my favorite breakfast diner, talking about everything and nothing at all, and it's… nice.

There are a lot of ways to a girl's heart, but to mine *specifically*?

Good taste in music, a new tattoo, or, in this case, a stack of double chocolate chip pancakes with extra whip cream.

And somehow, my favorite pancakes are inherently better when I'm sharing them with Davis Guidry.

Turns out my favorite chocolatey goodness is even better when I get them with a side of him. The guy with the bourbon eyes, chiseled jaw, and dimpled grin is nothing like I thought he'd be. He's not just stupidly handsome; he's funny, charming, and surprisingly sweet.

A lethal combination.

Our shoulders brush together when he throws his head back and laughs at one of my cheesy jokes, a delicious, deep, raspy sound that makes my stomach flip and my core clench at the same time.

"You know, watching you put down all those pancakes was possibly the hottest thing I've ever seen."

Honestly, this was the last place I expected him to take me, but it was a pleasant surprise. There's nothing better than pancakes for dinner, and we've spent the last hour laughing and getting to know each other... outside of the insane sexual chemistry we seem to share.

And I'm realizing how many things we actually have in common. How we both love trashy reality TV, '90s alternative, and sleeping in.

"What can I say? I have a healthy appetite."

He laughs with a nod. "Most girls are weird around guys when it comes to eating, or at least that's been my experience. To me, there's nothing sexier than a girl who eats. Cheeseburgers, pancakes, whatever. Fuck nothing but chicken and salad all the time."

"Nope, sorry. Not me." I shake my head. "I'm never passing up food if I'm hungry. And definitely not chocolate chip pancakes from Magnolia's. But I'm kinda surprised *you* ate them with all the syrup. My brother is so weird about everything he eats. Because of baseball, I guess?"

Davis nods. "Yeah. It's ninety-ten for me. Ninety percent of the time, I eat clean. I eat my protein, watch my sugar and carb intake. Follow the team dietician's plan. But then there's that ten percent where I indulge in stuff and allow myself to have something I'm craving. I make sure to keep up my workouts and not skip days even when I'm not eating a hundred percent clean." He reaches for the hem of his T-shirt and lifts, exposing his six-pack, shrugging. "I think it's working out."

I laugh. "Yeah, I'd say so."

Clearly, he has no issue with keeping his body looking the way that it does. He's got muscles in places that I literally do not even know how to pronounce, and every time I see them, my brain goes hazy for a few seconds.

Davis Guidry is the epitome of the female gaze.

"Gotta stop looking at me like that, babe."

Whoops. "Like what?" I ask, feigning innocence.

His lip curves into a lazy grin. "Like you want a repeat of your bedroom right in this parking lot."

We stay on the tailgate of his truck for what feels like hours talking, and I don't even realize how much time has passed until I'm yawning and my eyes have become heavy.

Davis notices and glances down at his watch, eyes widening. "Shit, we've been out here for two hours."

"I guess we got lost talking. You're easy to talk to, Loverboy, and honestly, I'll admit I'm surprised by how many things we actually have in common."

"You mean, besides how much we like to fuck each other?" he tests, his voice low and raspy. "Because I think that's something we're really good at together."

I roll my eyes, nudging his shoulder with mine. "Seriously though, I just guess I didn't think that this"—

I use my hand to gesture between us—"would require talking to each other or I guess…"

"Being friends?" he interjects, and I nod.

"Yeah."

"I told you I'm a likable guy, Trouble. It's impossible to not want to be my friend." His cocky smirk makes his dimples pop, and my heart does that thing where it flips and makes me breathless.

I should not be so affected by him, but he's right. He's impossible not to like, especially now that I know things about him. Like that his mom is his best friend, and he has a little brother who he FaceTimes every week and they watch *The Big Bang Theory* together. And how he keeps asking about my music, like those things are important to him. Those things make him more than just a hookup that leaves once it's over. It makes him more real.

"Mmm, I dunno. Jury's still out on that."

"Just give it time, babe. It's inevitable."

But… the truth is I don't need to give it any time because I already know just how likable he is, and that's what scares me the most.

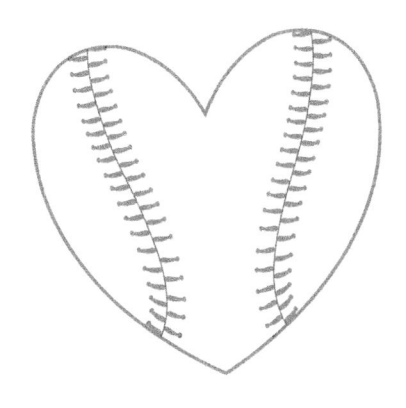

chapter ten

Davis

"Hotel"— Montell Fish

I knew this shit was going to happen eventually; I was just hoping he'd have time to simmer down and let this shit go, but clearly, that's not the case.

The moment Oliver sees me standing near my locker, he storms over, rage written all over his face. His hand flattens against the front of the locker as he slams it shut, barely missing my fingers. "I know what you're doing,

Guidry, and I'm warning you now... stay the fuck away from my sister. This is not a game. Zara is off-limits."

I don't immediately respond.

I say nothing because I'm choosing what to say next very carefully.

I'm *really* fucking into Zara, and I don't want to fuck that up having this shit with Oliver, but on the other hand, he's not my handler and sure as fuck isn't hers, and I've already had enough of this bullshit between us.

I'm not the one who feels threatened; it's him.

"You're the one with the problem, not me," I respond finally, tugging my clean T-shirt over my head. "I'm good."

He laughs humorlessly. "Yeah, I bet you're fucking good. Leave her out of this."

That's the second time he's insinuated that I'm seeing his sister just because of whatever problem he has with me, and fuck that.

"This bullshit between you and I has nothing to do with Zara. *You're* the one with an issue, not me. You truly don't even cross my fucking mind, Andrews. I don't owe you shit, and neither does she. She's a grown-up who can make her own decisions, but just so you know, I'm seeing her because I like her, not because it has shit to do with you."

"Oh, so you just *conveniently* decided to fuck with my sister, knowing the history that we have?"

I laugh. That only seems to piss him off more. "History? We're on the same fucking team, dude. The only history we have is you feeling threatened by the fact that you're up for the same starting spot I am, and Coach Baker is only going to pick one of us. You know, being an asshole and starting shit with me isn't going to get you any more ahead. It's based on the time we put in, how hard we work, if we're an asset to the team. *That's* what matters."

He knows it just as much as I do, and if he wants to have this conversation, then he needs to man the fuck up and discuss the real issue here. It's got nothing to do with Zara. Reaching down to the bench, I grab my phone and backpack before turning my attention back to him. "I have shit to do. See you around."

I turn and leave him standing there with his fists clenched at his side, looking even more pissed off than when he started this bullshit because I'm done with this conversation.

The only way I'm going to stop seeing Zara is if *she* makes that decision.

IT'S BEEN two weeks of me and Zara hooking up in secret, whenever and wherever we can.

Which hasn't been very easy since I always have a

house full of teammates, and she lives with her brother, but every chance we get, we're together. We meet at my apartment when everyone's gone or behind the arts building between classes. And no matter how much I have her, I still can't get enough of her.

It's never enough.

I want her from the moment I open my eyes, and most of the time, it's because she infiltrated my dreams, a constant presence even in my subconscious. Those fucking pretty red lips and bratty attitude that I can't ever decide if I want to spank or fuck out of her.

Both, in whatever order.

Today's secret meeting spot?

The piano studio that Zara rented to practice.

Absolutely not a place we should be hooking up in, but admittedly, it's kinda hot, the prospect of getting caught.

"Shhh, baby, you have to be quiet," I mumble against her pussy, reaching up to cover her mouth with my palm, stifling the sound.

She whimpers against my hand but nods, her eyes wild with lust.

Fuck, I wish her moans could echo off these walls like a goddamn symphony, the kind of composition only the two of us can create.

I glance around, finding the panties I pulled off her, and bring them to her mouth.

"If you're not quiet, then you don't get to come,

Trouble." My voice drops lower as I drag the lace over her plump, parted lips. "Only good girls get to come."

I gently shove the lace into her mouth until she's stuffed full of the wet lace that was just covering her pussy.

We said we weren't going to meet up anywhere that we could get caught, but she texted me earlier today with a picture of her bent over, wearing this short-as-fuck leather skirt with her panties tugged to the side to give me a glimpse of her pussy, and... well, you can probably guess how that ended.

With her splayed out on the back of this piano, my tongue deep in her pussy and her panties shoved in her mouth as a gag to keep her quiet.

Fuck, this girl makes me lose my head and do dumb shit, like eating her pussy in a room at school where any of the faculty could walk by at any moment.

"That's my good girl, taking my fingers so well." I know how much she loves when I praise her, a kink that we both share, and her pussy tightens around my fingers in response.

I bring my thumb up to circle her clit, thrumming the sensitive nub beneath my fingers like she's an instrument for me to play, pinching and rolling it until she's thrashing beneath me.

I can't devour her the way I want to with how quiet we need to be, so my licks are agonizingly slow and torturous, a pace that has us both dizzy with desperation. Fuck, I want to sink inside of her and fill her up, watch my cum pour out of her tight little hole.

Her fingers fly to my hair, tearing roughly at the strands as she falls apart beneath me, her inner walls squeezing my fingers, sending a gush of cum coating my tongue.

Goddamnit.

I can feel her entire body trembling from the power of her orgasm, and thank fucking fuck her panties are gagging her, or the entire city of New Orleans would know how good I am at eating my girl.

Well, she's not mine, but I don't know… maybe if she was, that wouldn't be a bad thing.

The thought surprises me, but I'm so lost in her that I don't even have time to really analyze what it means.

"I brought you a surprise," I murmur, rising to my knees between her thighs and wiping the excess of her cum off my lips with the back of my hand. "You told me last night you wanted to try something…"

Trailing off, I reach into the pocket of my jeans and pull out the small butt plug I got for her, lifting it for her to see. Last night, when we were on FaceTime, she mentioned how much she loves when I stick my finger in her ass, and when I asked if she wanted to go any further with it, she rolled her lip between her teeth and gave me the sexiest fucking nod I've ever seen.

I swear I almost came in my pants imagining her

bent over, taking my cock in her perfect, heart-shaped ass.

Fuckkkk. Me.

Which is why I immediately went to the nearest Hustler and spent thirty minutes picking out the perfect plug for her, to loosen her up so she can eventually take my cock. The plug is small and black, with a gem at the base that's almost exactly the same shade of red as her lipstick that I love so goddamn much. When I saw it, I knew it was perfect for her. And I couldn't wait to see it inside her.

Her eyes widen slightly when she sees me twirl it between my fingers, and my lip curves.

She looks surprised, but I can see the flicker of excitement burning in her eyes.

"What do you say we play, Trouble?"

I watch as her throat bobs, a rough swallow as her wild, heated gaze drops from me to the plug, and then she nods. With my free hand, I gently pull the panties from her mouth. "Consent is everything, baby. Need to hear you say it."

"Yes," she mumbles breathlessly with a nod.

"Tell me you want this plug in your ass," I whisper, bringing it to her lips and dragging along her bottom lip.

Her fingers curl around my wrist. "I want you to use it." Then she wraps her lips around the small plug, sucking it into her mouth and twirling her tongue around it while she holds my gaze.

Motherfucker, I think I like this girl.

My throat bobs as a wave of lust washes over me. She knows exactly what she's doing to me.

She pulls her lips off the plug with a pop and reaches for my jeans, hooking her fingers in the waistband and hauling me closer until her hot little pussy is pressed against me, leaving behind a wet spot.

"Well, are you going to stand there, or are you going to fuck my ass, Davis?"

She flicks the button of my jeans open, dragging the zipper down until the fabric hangs open. My cock is straining against my boxers, the angry, red head peeking from the waistband, and when she sees the precum coating my slit, her eyes flood with heat.

I slide my hand around the back of her neck and crash my lips to hers, slipping my tongue into her mouth and kissing all the sass right off her lips, letting her taste herself on my tongue.

She's a brat, but fuck, she's *my* brat.

"Gonna fuck you right where you make your music, Zara. Every time you're in here after this, I want you to think about how you came on my cock. How I filled both your tight little ass and your pussy at the same time."

I spread her thighs wider, exposing her glistening cunt. Pretty and pink, so swollen from my lips that it makes my cock weep. I slide two fingers into her, gathering her wetness on the tips and bringing it to her asshole, coating the tight ring in preparation for the plug. My thumb circles her clit as I push my finger into her ass. Only the tip.

Her breath hitches, and then she whimpers loudly. The sound echoes off the walls, and I grab the panties, shoving them back into her mouth.

"Quiet, Trouble, or I'll leave you empty and desperate to come. Be my good girl."

A hungry, dark look passes over her face, and I smirk, pushing my finger in further, burying it to the knuckle as I massage her clit.

When she starts to relax, I add another finger, fucking her with both at once. Her hips roll as she arches her back, pressing her clit against my thumb and my fingers deeper into her ass. I rub the swollen bud in soft circles, slowly until I feel her muscles going lax.

I spit on her pussy, watching it trail down, covering her clit and dripping all the way to where my fingers are buried inside of her ass. Withdrawing them, I spread the wetness around her hole, then push my fingers deep, all the way to the hilt, before pulling them out and this time replacing them with the plug.

While steadily stroking her clit, I slowly push the plug through the tight ring of resistance until the tip slips inside.

It's a little bigger than my fingers, but fuck, she takes it so good.

"That's it, baby, relax," I breathe, bending to suck her clit into my mouth, rolling it between my lips.

Even with her mouth full, she cries out, falling flat against the piano, jostling it slightly. She's so responsive, and it's fucking amazing the way she melts just for me.

A few flicks of my tongue and a little more languid pressure, and the plug is buried to the base, with Zara writhing between me, on the brink of another orgasm.

I drag my fingers through her soaked cunt, coating my fingers and palm before I grab my cock. I grip the base, squeezing roughly before pumping and fucking my fist.

With how hard I am, I could blow right now just looking at her slick pussy spread open in front of me and the red gem peeking out from between her asscheeks.

Her thigh hitches on my side as I press the thick head of my cock to her entrance, dragging the tip against her clit a few times and then slowly pushing inside.

"You're doing so good, baby. Are you going to be my good girl and come on my cock just like you did my fingers?"

She nods over and over as I thrust deep inside her to the hilt, my cock buried in her pussy and the plug stretching her ass.

Rookie Mistake

I can feel it pressing against my cock as her walls squeeze me, sucking me deeper into her greedy cunt. Her clit brushes against the short hair at my pelvis, and her fingers fly to my stomach, digging into the muscles as she writhes.

Nothing will ever feel as perfect as she does, and I realize I might be more than a tad bit fucked when it comes to this girl. Stilling inside of her, I give her a second to adjust to the new feeling of both of her holes full of me. I breathe through my nose so I don't come because I need her to come again before I do. Everything in my body is tight, all of my muscles coiling as I fight for control.

If there is a heaven, it's right the fuck here, buried inside Zara.

"You okay?" I rasp.

When she nods and hooks a leg behind my ass, pulling me deeper into her, I smirk.

My crazy, dirty fucking girl.

Dipping my head, I push her shirt up to yank the cup of her bra down, sucking her nipple into my mouth and biting gently, using my teeth on the sensitive peak.

Biting back my own groan, I slowly start to move, dragging my cock out of her and slamming it back inside as she soaks me in her juices and moans around the panties in her mouth.

I wish we were someplace more private so I could take my time, drag this out, bring her to the edge of orgasm over and over, keeping it just out of reach, edging her until she was limp and boneless beneath me. But we only have so long before her studio time is up, so this has to be fast.

So I give in to our hunger, fucking her so hard that the keys on the piano shake, creating a cacophony of sounds that echoes throughout the room. My thrusts are slow and deep, bottoming out inside of her with each snap of my hips. Sweat drips from my forehead onto her chest, and I lean down, dragging my tongue along her skin, licking it up, and biting her nipples. With each thrust of my hips, I feel the plug pressing against her inner walls.

"Look at your greedy little pussy taking my cock while your ass stretches around that plug, sucking it in. My dirty girl," I pant.

When I bring my thumb back to her clit, rubbing fast, quick circles, I feel her tightening around my cock, moments from an orgasm. And even though I wish I could make this last, I slam my hips, planting my cock deep in her as I follow her over the edge into oblivion.

Her fingers dig into my back as her hips roll to meet mine, pushing my cock even deeper in her as I fill her with my cum.

"Fuck," I grunt, dropping my forehead to her stomach as her pussy wrings every drop of cum out of me. My thrusts slow, but the erratic beat of my heart seems to quicken.

I feel her fingers tangle into my hair, dragging lazily through the strands as we both attempt to catch our breath. I lift my head and peer down at her. Her cheeks are flushed and her lips swollen from mine, and she's never looked more gorgeous.

"Trying to kill me, Trouble," I murmur, gently pulling out of her.

My cum drips out of her glistening pussy, but I gather it on my fingers and push it back inside of her, not missing the way she tightens around them.

I pull my hand free and reach for her panties, tugging them out of her mouth and replacing them with my fingers. She hungrily sucks them, cleaning both of our cum from the digits.

My dick twitches, and I swear if I hadn't just filled her with my cum, I'd be hard again.

"Are you okay?"

"Yep," she says with a small smile. "Thanks for the hot sex and two orgasms."

I lift a brow. "You mean three?"

"Who's keeping count?" she retorts sassily.

"Brat."

Her grin is cheeky as she says, "But... what about the plug?"

Hm.

"You can wear it to class. That way, you won't forget who just fucked the shit out of you. And these?" I say, lifting her panties. "I think I'll keep these. You can sit through class with my plug in your ass and my cum dripping out of your pussy."

Her eyes flare with heat. "No way."

I chuckle. "Oh? Remember, Trouble, only good girls get to come. Might wanna be a good girl if you want my *cock* in your ass next time."

She rolls her eyes as a small smirk turns the corner of her pillowy lip up, but unsurprisingly, the girl who always has something to say… is perfectly quiet.

Since she's quiet, I use the moment to kiss her, reminding her of all the reasons why being a good girl is so much more fun.

chapter eleven

Zara

"Goosebumps"— HVME

Another night, another party at the Kappa house. Still not my favorite place to be on a Saturday night, but Harper dragged me and Lily here tonight.

But tonight, Oliver and Davis are *both* in attendance, which means that I have to pretend like we haven't been sneaking around for the last few weeks behind my brother's back and having the best sex of my life.

Absolute torture seeing as how Davis looks so

fucking hot standing across the living room in loose, faded jeans, a black baseball T-shirt stretched across his broad chest with a hat turned backward.

He's giving 2000s Heath Ledger, and my mouth is *watering*.

I bring the Solo cup to my lips and take a small sip, staring over the rim at Davis, dragging my gaze down his body.

God, I'm so horny for him it's ridiculous. No matter how many times we hook up and he does delicious, dirty things to my body, I still want more.

"Hate to break it you, babe, but you two are *so* obvious," Harper whispers matter-of-factly from beside me with a smirk. "I think the only person who *doesn't* see you making googly eyes at each other from across the room is Oliver."

My gaze whips to my best friend. "Not true. I'm just… admiring the view."

"Sorry, Zar, but that guy is staring at you like he's the big bad wolf and you're his next meal," Lily adds from my other side, agreeing with Harper.

I turn back toward Davis and find him looking directly at me, his eyes dark and hungry as they slip down my body, a lazy grin plastered on his pillowy lips. My skin hums as he does a slow perusal, pausing his gaze where my dress stops high on my thighs and imperceptibly shaking his head as he darts his tongue out and licks his lip.

I may have worn this dress knowing he'd be here tonight, just to tease him. And so when he finally gets his hands on me, it'll be my favorite, unhinged, absolutely filthy version of him.

Fine.

We're totally eye-fucking each other, but as long as my brother doesn't pick up on that little tidbit, then we're good.

"Have you seen him? It's not like I'm in control here. My vagina has a mind of her own, and the only thing she wants is him," I respond with a shrug, taking another sip of my drink. It's only my first, but the alcohol already has my limbs feeling loose and heavy, and now I want to dance. "Come dance with me."

We replenish our drinks and head to the dance floor, and I force myself to spend time with my girls and not look for Davis.

If there's one thing Kappa is good for aside from the free, cheap liquor, it's their playlists. Some places play lame shit, but they always have the good stuff.

"Cruel Summer" plays through the speakers, and we dance together, jumping up and down, swaying to the beat, giggling when Harper breaks out some ridiculous dance moves that are atrocious at best.

These are my favorite nights. The ones where we're all together, laughing, having the time of our lives. The nights I'll look back on when we graduate and all head off into the real world.

With my arms lifted in the air, I sway my hips to the beat, my eyes dropping closed as I lose myself in the music.

Suddenly, I feel the heat of a body behind me and an unfamiliar voice near my ear. "Damn, baby, you look hot as fuck in that dress." An arm snakes around my waist, hauling me backward, and when I glance behind me, I see a tall, blond guy who I don't know.

"Not interested, pal, sorry," I clip as I pull his arm off my waist and step away. But idiot stranger pulls me back, locking his arm back around my waist, holding me tightly against him.

"Don't fucking touch me."

I can smell the foul stench of alcohol on him, and even if he wasn't being a handsy asshole, the smell alone would be enough for me not to want to be anywhere in the vicinity of him.

Guys can be such dicks.

I'm whipping around to tell him to fuck right off when suddenly, he's gone, the smell of stale beer and cheap liquor lingering in the air between us. I turn and see Davis standing there, his jaw clenched so tightly it looks like it's going to snap.

His eyes are dark and full of fury as he uses both hands to shove idiot stranger backward, where he stumbles and topples to the floor. "She said don't fucking touch her. Got a hearing problem or just a drunk asshole problem?"

Holy. Fuck.

God, how is he even hotter right now? Violence doesn't normally do it for me, but a possessive, angry Davis absolutely does.

His chest is heaving as he stands between us, pushing me behind him with one big, shaking palm.

The drunk idiot on the ground raises his hands in surrender as he scrambles away from Davis, the crowd parting for the fight that's about to happen. I drag my gaze from him and scan the crowd for Oliver, thankfully not finding him anywhere.

"Hey, man, I didn't mean anything. I just wanted to dance with her," the guy stutters, and Davis takes a menacing step forward.

"Yeah, well, when a woman says don't fucking touch her, then you *don't* fucking touch her, dickhead."

I can feel the situation escalating by the second, palpable tension hanging in the air around us, so I step between them, sliding my palms along the smooth skin of Davis's biceps. His gaze darts down to me as he breathes heavily. I watch the muscle in his jaw ripple as he clenches his teeth together, his hands fisted tightly at his sides.

"Hey. Hey. Look at me," I say as I bring my hand to his jaw to cup it, sweeping my thumb along his jawline. "He's not worth it." His jaw clenches beneath my hand, and I continue to stroke his skin, rising on my tiptoes to place my lips as close to his ear as I can. He needs a distraction; I can feel the fury still rolling off him, and I have the perfect one. "If you could only feel how wet I am right now. I'm so hot for you right now, Davis Guidry."

A low chuckle vibrates from his chest, and I smirk, pulling back to gaze up at him. Finally, I feel his anger starting to disappear. He shoots one last murderous look at the guy behind me, but I guide his face back to me. "How about we go somewhere and I can show you just how much you being all possessive just turned me on?"

His eyes flare, and his lip curves up. "Meet me on the third floor. Last door to the right."

I nod and turn to head in that direction, but his hand catches mine, stopping me. "Bring my favorite lipstick, Trouble."

A shiver runs down my spine, and my nipples pebble as his words wash over me.

Unhinged, *filthy* Davis is here, and he's ready to play.

I WOULDN'T CALL myself obedient. Not by a long shot. I've always been the kind of girl who thrives on chaos, anarchy, defiance. It's in my blood.

That is until Davis Guidry.

I'm currently on my knees, my hands resting on his thighs as he stares down at me. Anticipation snakes heavily down my spine while my thighs are pressed tightly together, an attempt at dulling the steady ache inside my core.

"Good girl. You wore it," he rasps darkly, the rough pad of his thumb dragging along my lower lip and smearing his favorite lipstick. YSL Le Rouge, my signature color. The one he's been *obsessed* with since the night we met.

The throbbing in my clit intensifies with his praise, and I realize in this moment just how obedient I'd be for this man, in whatever he asked for.

"You look so fucking pretty on your knees for me, Zara. My dick is already hard as fuck," he murmurs.

When I brush my fingers over his erection, he hisses and clenches his teeth, those tight muscles in his jaw working with the motion. After the fight that almost happened earlier, I can feel the adrenaline still coursing through him. The slightest tremble to his muscles as if he's holding on to a small, fraying thread of restraint.

I want it to break, letting out the man lurking beneath the surface.

A piece of him reserved only for me.

I'm so fucking hot for him that it feels as if I'm burning from the inside out. My skin is ablaze as he trails his fingers lower until he curves his palm around my throat, squeezing lightly.

In response, I flick the button of his jeans open and slowly drag the zipper down, holding his smoldering gaze. I grip his erection through the thin fabric of his briefs until his hold on my throat tightens, the pressure from his fingers intensifying until my heart begins to race.

"Take my cock out, Zara."

Heat floods my lower belly as I tug his briefs lower, inch by inch, freeing his straining cock. Thick and long, it's the perfect dick. Just the right amount of girth, with a thick vein running down the length.

My mouth actually waters, and I can't wait another second to have him in my mouth. Leaning forward, I circle the base and close my lips over the head, sucking just the tip.

A tease of what's to come.

The salty, musky taste of his precum floods my tongue, and I moan around him.

He groans, a deep, guttural noise from the back of his throat as he threads his fingers into my hair.

I don't dare close my eyes because there is nothing sexier than this man being overcome by pleasure.

Pleasure from *me*.

I've never felt so powerful in my life.

His eyes are dark and stormy, heavy with need, his lips parted as he watches me take him deeper into my mouth.

He's *enchanted*.

This is his fantasy, one that we've talked about in length, and I'm all too happy to give it to him.

It's one of my favorite things about what we're doing. That we're open and honest about what we want and the things that turn us on and get us off. It's been so much fun exploring things with him.

I let the head of his cock slip out of my mouth with a pop as I drag my tongue along the prominent vein from tip to root and back. His hand bracketing my throat tightens, and he groans, "Fuuuck, Zara. You have no idea how long I've wanted to see those pretty lips circling my cock, painting it red."

I bring my palm to his balls, cupping, rolling, tugging them lightly at the same time I suck him back into my mouth, taking him deep until he hits the back of my throat. Because I'm not blessed with a no-gag reflex, I choke around him, my eyes watering in the process.

His fingers thread into my hair roughly, guiding me up and down on his cock, his hips flexing as he fucks my throat in short, choppy movements, showing just how out of control he is tonight.

It's the absolute hottest moment of my life.

He's using my mouth, making me feel dirty in the best way, and I can't get enough.

Tears and saliva stream down my face when he thrusts deep, holding my mouth down on his cock as he grunts, "Put your fingers in your panties and rub your clit while I come down your throat."

I follow directions like the obedient girl I'm being tonight, dipping my fingers inside the waistband of my panties, finding my clit swollen and throbbing just from sucking his dick. My hips jolt when the pad of my finger brushes over it, and I circle my finger, trying not to pass out from the pleasure rippling through me.

"Fuck, look at you, Zara. On your knees, getting your face fucked. Smearing those red lips all over my cock like a good girl. I can't get enough."

Withdrawing, he slams his hips forward with a deep, guttural groan, the head of his cock hitting the back of my throat again.

Pinching my clit between my fingers, I can't hold back the orgasm that shoots through me like a rocket, my hips shaking as I try to remain on my knees and not slide to the floor.

"Coming, baby. Fuckkkkk, I'm coming," Davis pants, holding the top of my head and my chin as he rocks his hips deep. I feel his warm cum sliding down my throat as he erupts, emptying every drop down my throat.

I swallow it down greedily, moaning from the overwhelming sensation of coming while having him fuck my mouth.

Jesus, that was hot. So hot that even after coming... I still want more.

He pulls his cock out of my mouth, watching the trail of saliva trail from my mouth, his eyes darkening.

"You are the hottest fucking creature alive. You did

so well taking my cock," he praises, leaning forward and capturing my lips, uncaring that there are tears and smeared lipstick all over my face. If anything, I think it turns him on more. "Your turn. Take off your panties and get on the bed. I want to fucking drown in your pussy, Zara."

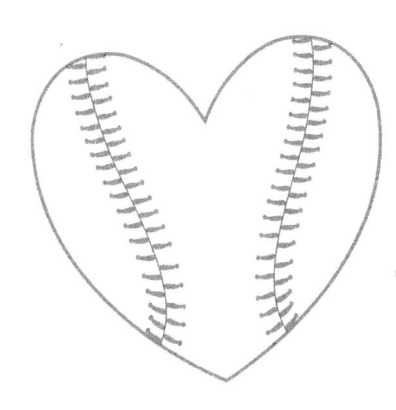

chapter twelve
Davis

"Again"— Noah Cyrus

I can hardly walk as I make my way back out to the party because she sucked the fucking soul out of me through the head of my cock.

I'm like a newborn goddamn foal pushing through the crowd in search of my teammates.

I didn't want to leave her after we met in the bedroom, but she said she wanted to touch up her makeup with Harper and Lily, and that's fair since I smeared that red lipstick all over her when I fucked her face.

Fuck, I almost lost my head tonight when I saw that guy with his hands on her.

Not just because he was *touching* her but because he was touching her without her permission, *after* she told him to get his goddamn hands off her.

Only an asshole touches a woman without her permission, and I wanted to fuck him up I was so pissed off, fuck every single one of the consequences.

My pitching hand being the consequence, and also potentially my place on the team, so part of me was thankful that Zara intervened when she did before I ruined my baseball career over that dickhead.

But I would have. For her.

The house is packed tonight, and it takes forever for me to make it to the kitchen to get a drink because I keep getting stopped by everyone. But my mind's not really there. Not after what just happened with Zara and everything that's happened tonight.

I've never really been a relationship kind of guy, but I feel like maybe that's starting to change.

Fuck, I almost killed that asshole tonight, all because he touched her. And not just because he did it without her consent.

Yeah, that alone would have been enough for me to

beat the shit out of him, but in that moment, I realized I don't want *anyone* touching Zara.

The thought of Zara touching anyone else, or anyone touching her, sends jealousy coursing through my veins in a torrential wave.

A feeling I never thought I'd experience because I honestly never thought I'd find anyone who would make me want to have more than one night.

More than friends who *occasionally* hook up.

Until I met Zara.

It's fucking scary because this was supposed to be no strings attached, a friend-with-benefits kind of thing, but I haven't even looked at another girl since I met her. I haven't wanted to.

Clearly, that means something. We're more than friends who just hook up… I don't know what it is exactly that I want, but what I do know is that I'm not ready for this to end. I want to be selfish and keep her all to myself for as long as she'll let me.

"Rookie, what up, my man," my teammate Theo yells when I walk into the crowded dining room area where the tables have been converted into a heated beer pong tournament.

I walk over to him, taking the blue Solo cup of alcohol he's handing me before we shake hands. "What's up?"

He shrugs as I take a sip, swallowing down the burn of vodka. "Same ole, you know. Ready for baseball to start. I think we've got a good shot this year against Alabama. I can't stand those assholes."

The rivalry that would withstand time, all thanks to Nick Saban.

"Yeah, I think so too," I respond, dragging my attention over to the beer pong table, where a few of my teammates are playing, along with a few guys from the football and hockey teams. I lift a hand, waving to Bennett Breaux, the hockey team's enforcer. We've crossed paths a few times, and the guy is legit the surliest, grumpiest guy I've ever met, but we're still cordial to each other since we run in the same circles.

"You hear from Grant lately?" Theo asks, referencing my best friend, who recently graduated and is playing for the Sea Dogs.

I nod. "Yeah, we text during the week, and he FaceTimed me the other day."

The truth is I miss the shit out of him. I miss pissing him off because he's uptight as fuck, and I miss having him to shoot the shit with about nothing. No one warns you before going to college that you get close to people, and then they abandon you.

Fine, not abandon—graduate, but it's basically the same thing.

We start talking about who we're drafting for the team's fantasy football league this year when someone checks me from behind so hard that I nearly fall over, only catching myself last minute on the wall in front of me before I end up on the floor.

Alcohol splashes over the rim of my cup, all over the front of my T-shirt and jeans, completely soaking my clothes.

What the fuck?

Turning, I see Oliver fucking Andrews standing behind me, wearing a sinister smirk. His green eyes, I'm now realizing since we're standing so close, resemble the same bright emerald as his sister's.

"What the fuck, Andrews?" I spit as I toss my empty cup onto a nearby table. There's nothing left now that I'm fucking wearing it.

"You just couldn't stay away, could you?" He steps closer until the tips of his shoes meet mine and shoves me with both hands. My back slams against the wall with a loud thud that sounds around the room, even over the sound of music pouring from the speakers.

This *motherfucker*.

I'm going from never getting in fights to almost getting into two tonight. 2 and 0.

"I told you to stay away from Zara. I fucking warned you what would happen if you continued, and you didn't give a shit. You did it anyway. I told you she was off-fucking-limits, but you just couldn't help yourself."

I just shake my fucking head because I'm in disbelief that this shit is evening happening right now. He must have seen us going upstairs together earlier, even though we thought we were being so careful... But fine, if this is what he wants to do, then let's fucking go.

"And I'm pretty sure I recall telling you to mind your own fucking business. You don't make decisions for her, Oliver." I shove him back, not hard enough to knock him on his ass, but hard enough that he stumbles back a few steps. "You sure you wanna do this right now? Right here?"

A dark shadow of determination passes over his face, and he nods, closing the distance between us. "What I want is to fuck you up for touching my sister. I warned you, and you didn't give a shit. I told you this wasn't a game, Guidry. She is my fucking sister, and she is not some toy you can use and throw away when you're done."

"You think I don't know that?" I retort darkly. "Just because you have an opinion about who you think I am doesn't mean I treat Zara with anything less than what she deserves. It's disrespectful as fuck that you're the one here causing a scene instead of talking to me man to man about it."

"Nothing to talk about. You're not fucking with my sister, end of discussion."

This time, I chuckle. The sound is completely humorless and more so to keep me from breaking his nose.

I'm fucking done with this shit, and I'm done with him.

This is the second time we've had this conversation,

and nothing has changed. Except maybe my feelings about Zara, and it still has fuck all to do with him.

The fact that he keeps letting the bullshit rivalry as a reason to start shit with me is pissing me the fuck off. Sure, I don't like him and probably never will, but this shit has gone too far. How are we supposed to perform as a team if we can't even stand to be in the same room, if we're fighting over shit at frat parties?

We'll be fucked this season, even if it were both up for the same spot. One of us will be a relief pitcher for the other, and the entire team doesn't jive if guys are at each other's throats.

Fuck this.

"Let's end this shit, right here," I tell him, lifting my chin. "You wanna beat the shit out of me for wanting to be with Zara? Fine. Do it, then get the fuck over it and move on because I'm not going to stop. I know you have a low opinion of me and think I'm just out to fuck her, but that's not true. I like her, Oliver, and I want to do shit the right way. So get your anger out, let's throw a few punches, and move. The. Fuck. On."

I punctuate every syllable, watching his expression change from anger to red-hot fury.

I continue, letting the attention we've garnered fade out. "How do you think this is going to end? Both of us benched for the first game? A suspension from the team for who knows how long? Maybe Coach deciding that neither of us are worth the trouble and giving the starting spot to Rio instead. Maybe you don't care, but this shit has to end. Tonight. So let's do whatever the fuck we can to make sure that happens. Hit me. Do your fucking worst."

I'm taunting him.

Goading him into taking the first punch.

Hopefully, it makes him feel better and resolves whatever is happening in his head because neither of us are walking out of here without ending this shit.

For a beat, he doesn't move. He doesn't speak, he doesn't even fucking breathe by the looks of it, his eyes boring into the hardwood at my feet, and then he drags his gaze to meet mine. "You could've picked anyone in the goddamn world, and you picked my sister. You're a selfish fuck. You're willing to hurt Zara just to get to me. "

Fuck this.

I stride toward him, my steps short as I close the distance and shove him hard. "Fuck you. She's not a goddamn game to me, and I'm fucking sick of hearing you talk about her like she's not capable of making her own decisions. Leave her out of this. You say this bullshit is because of me and her, but let's be real for one second. It's not. This is about you feeling threatened that I'll take the starting spot."

I've been so caught up in the fact that I'm about to potentially fight my teammate and the stupid shit that's coming out of his mouth that I didn't catalog how much of a crowd has gathered around us. Aside from the music still playing, most of the party has gone silent, watching us circling each other.

Great. It'll take one person recording a video for social media, and both of us will be fucked. Coach has been cracking down on us for social media practices, and that's why I've been working so hard to clean my act up so he sees that I'm serious about wanting to earn my spot as a starter.

"I think it's *you* that feels threatened, Guidry. As much as you bring up that starting spot, seems like you're scared that you're not good enough to get it." He smirks as he dips a shoulder. "Damn, it looks like you're not getting that spot or my fucking sister. Asshole."

He pushes me again, and this time when I return the smile, he rears back and punches me. For a six-foot-two, two-hundred-pound guy, he moves fast as fuck. I barely have time to move before his knuckles land on my brow bone, splitting it open as I stagger back, hitting the wall.

Immediately, I feel the trickle of warm, wet blood as it trails down the spot above my eye and onto my cheek.

The crowd starts chanting, "Fight, fight, fight."

My adrenaline is fucking pumping, and my vision is hazy from anger, and right now, with as mad as I am, I feel like saying fuck the consequences.

Reaching up, I swipe the blood off my face and wipe it onto my jean-covered thighs.

"You wanted a fight, so here you fucking go. Now,

hit me back," he taunts, stepping up to me, his chest bumping mine.

I don't even have a chance to return the punch because a five-foot-nothing spitfire with midnight hair and bright green eyes that always seem to take hold of my throat steps between us. "What in the *fuck* is going on?"

chapter thirteen

Zara

"Power Trip"— J.Cole, Miguel

I don't think I've ever been so angry in my entire life.

Actually, angry doesn't even touch what I'm feeling right now. *Stabby* is more like it, and I'm pretty positive my brother is going to be the recipient of said anger.

Davis has blood pouring from a cut above his eye, and Oliver has the audacity to look guilty, and I know that he's the one that caused all of this since he's not the one bleeding.

I don't doubt that Davis participated in whatever happened, but for it to resort to physical violence? No.

Hell no.

"I cannot believe you *hit* him, Oliver!" I hiss, trying to keep my fiery temper under bay. Sucking in a deep breath that's meant to calm me, but no such luck, I exhale through my nose. "I want to talk to you both. Not here."

It's at that moment that my idiot brother does a slow scan of the crowd that's gathered around them as if he's just now realizing that he's acted like a complete fool in front of hundreds of people with their phones out. His throat bobs as he swallows, and he nods. I then look over at Davis, who also nods, and I brush past them, pushing through the throng of people toward the back door of the Kappa house.

Once we're outside, I glance around the backyard and see that even though it's not empty, it's not nearly as packed as the inside of the house, and it gives us a bit more privacy. This conversation is happening either way, but I don't want to do it in front of an entire frat house full of drunk people.

I whip to face Oliver, months of pent-up frustration and exhaustion finally boiling over. He's got his hands shoved into the pockets of his jeans, a contrite expression on his face, and it only makes me more angry. "I can't believe that you did this, Oliver. It's low, even for you. I told you that I didn't want you getting involved in my personal life, and what do you do? Get into a fight with someone I'm seeing. Not only did you completely disregard every single thing that I asked you, you jeopardized *both* of your careers when Davis has done *nothing* wrong. You really said fuck my boundaries, huh? They don't mean shit to you and your agenda. It just shows me that you have no respect for me."

I realized that I'm not just angry that my brother hit Davis or that, once again, he's trying to control my life and make decisions for me, but his stupid decisions affect us all, not only him. "Are you okay?" I ask Davis, reaching out and grasping his chin so I can turn his face to the side and get a better look at the cut.

He nods. "Yeah, Trouble, I'm good."

"Okay. Can you give me a second?" I say quietly.

For a second, he hesitates, as if he wants to make sure I'm okay, but when I nod, he says, "Yeah, of course."

He gives me a small smile before walking over off the back porch and into the yard.

I turn back to face Oliver, who's now strangely silent when just moments ago, he had so much to say inside the house. "I'm tired, Oliver. I'm seriously just exhausted from doing this, and tonight was the final straw. I can't and won't keep doing this fighting with you. Even if it wasn't Davis, it would be someone els—"

"Zara, he's a fucking prick, and I told you that you can't keep seeing him!" he interjects, his voice shaking with anger.

My brow quirks, tense silence lingering heavily between us. After a beat passes, I step forward until I'm nearly chest to chest with my brother, even if he's six two, and I'm five two in combat boots. My attitude is six five, and if there's anyone who knows not to push me to this point, it's him. And now that he has, he's going to listen to what I have to say. "Look, I understand you want to protect me and that when I dated one of your teammates in the past that it didn't end great, but that doesn't mean that you get to boss me around and try to control me." Pausing, I shake my head. "We had this same conversation weeks ago, and you clearly didn't hear a word I said. So, I'm done. I'm packing my stuff, and I'm going to stay with Harper. Indefinitely. And don't worry, I'll call Dad, too, and have the same conversation with him. Neither of you are going to make decisions for me. Behaving like this? Acting fucking insane and fighting people? That's how you lose me forever."

His eyes widen in disbelief. "Zar, you can't just *move out*. I'm supposed to look out for you, an—"

"Yeah, and smothering me until I can't breathe is your equivalent of 'looking after me,' Oliver," I cry, cutting him off. "Seriously, please listen to what I'm saying. You're my brother, and I love you. But you're suffocating me, and I can't do it anymore. You aren't protecting me; you're *hurting* me. I'm going home to pack my stuff. I want you to leave. This conversation is over."

Oliver's jaw clenches, and then his mouth opens like he wants to say something, but he closes it and then turns on his heel and disappears back inside the frat house.

I take a second to get myself together, brushing my hands down the front of my skirt. I'm so frustrated and honestly so embarrassed by what happened tonight. It's the second time my brother has embarrassed me with Davis, and I'm really over apologizing for Oliver's behavior.

I blow out a breath before turning to walk down the steps to the backyard. I see Davis standing near the fence, scrolling on his phone. He glances up as I approach, and I roll my lips together, scrunching my nose.

"I'm sorry. I feel like I keep having to say that when it comes to my brother, and I realize that he needs to be the one apologizing, but I'm so sorry, Davis. I can't believe he hit you," I whisper, stepping closer, shame lacing my words.

My brother, the psycho.

Has a ring to it, I think.

"Don't apologize. Sure, he started it, but I was talking just as much shit as he was. We've got our own shit to work out."

I nod, reaching up to brush my thumb near the cut, shaking my head. "Yeah, but he should have never hit you."

"Guys fight. It's what we do."

"I just don't want you to get into trouble with your coach for fighting. People had their phones out."

Davis's shoulder dips in a shrug. "It'll work itself out. I'm sure Coach will make us run till we puke, but it's not the first time someone from the team has fought, and I'm sure it won't be the last."

"You know, you're being strangely blasé about all of this," I say as I cross my arms over my chest, a teasing smile curving my lips. "I honestly expected you to be, I don't know, angry? My brother punched you."

"I probably would've punched him back if you hadn't shown up. I was pissed, but it doesn't really do any good to be mad about it. If shit hits the fan with Coach, then I'll cross that bridge when I get there."

"I may have overheard some of the conversation before punches were thrown." I grin, peering up at him through my lashes. He reaches for me and places his hand at my waist, sliding it to the small of my back before he pulls me toward him slowly.

There's a hint of a smile on his pillowy lips. "Yeah?"

I hum. "Mhmm. Something about you... liking me? Maybe?"

He chuckles, and the sound causes a flutter in my stomach. I've decided I like that sound way too much. "Maybe. I guess that depends on whether or not you feel the same way."

The truth is I asked myself the same question, and then I realized... there has never been a time since meeting Davis that I didn't like him. That he didn't make me laugh or make me look forward to opening a text message from him. I've spent the last few weeks deliriously happy, and so the answer to that question is definitely yes.

It was supposed to be one spontaneous, fun night that has turned out to be so much more.

"And if I do?"

His smirk widens into a smile, that dimple popping in his cheek with the motion. "Then, I'd say that I wanna date you, Trouble. I wanna take you to dinner, hold your hand and not give a shit who sees it. Kiss you in the quad, take you to parties and the entire room knows that you're mine. I told your brother that I liked you, and I meant it. I know that we said no strings, no feelings, but that didn't exactly go as planned."

He's not wrong. *He* doesn't fit into the plan I had for my freshman year of college, but then again, I've never really been great with plans.

I shrug. "Well, plans are overrated. Look at the night

that I bid on you here at this very house. Everything about that night was spontaneous, and it was one of the best nights I've ever had. Who cares if it's not part of the plan... because I don't. I like you too, Loverboy, and if you want to date me, then I accept. But I have to ask that our first official date be at Magnolia's. It's only fitting, don't you think?"

Davis nods. "Whatever my girlfriend wants, she gets."

"Oh... is that what we're calling this? Sounds *very* official," I tease as I run my fingers along his jawline before I slide them into the hair at his nape.

"Yeah, I know you have that commitment problem, but sorry, Trouble..." He dips his head until his lips are a centimeter from mine, and I can smell the sweet scent of mint lingering on his breath. "I don't share."

"Perfect, because neither do I."

He chuckles against my mouth before his lips crash into mine, kissing me until my legs feel like they'll give out from the fire spreading through me like wildfire. His tongue sweeps into my mouth, teasing, stroking, taking anything and everything that I have to give.

It feels different than any kiss we've shared before. Maybe because now... he's mine.

Davis pulls back, cradling my cheeks in his palms as he stares down at me and gives me my favorite, flirty smile.

"I wanna scream about you from the rooftop, Trouble. What do you say about me introducing you to my friends? Officially."

It's been a crazy, emotional night, but somehow, just these few moments with Davis make me feel so much better. Just being around his laid-back, easygoing attitude brings me a sense of calm I didn't even know how badly I needed.

"I would love that," I say quietly against his lips.

His smirk widens into the most gorgeous smile that makes the dimple in his cheek pop. He laces our fingers together, then says, "Then let's go, Trouble."

chapter fourteen
Zara

"Nothing's Gonna Hurt You Baby"— Cigarettes After Sex

It takes less than twenty-four hours after moving into Harper's dorm for my brother to show up at her door. I guess he really didn't believe me when I said that I would pack all of my stuff and leave. Because I did, and even though I'm sleeping on Harper's lumpy, slightly smelly old couch for the foreseeable future, it's *still* better than dealing with Oliver on the daily.

I don't regret my decision in the least, even though he's standing here looking like a kicked puppy.

Crossing my arms over my chest, I pop a brow. "What are you doing here?"

"I... came to apologize. To you. Not to him," he says with a sheepish expression.

My eyes roll as I reach for the door and curve my palm around the handle. "You're off to a great start, Oliver. Truly."

"Fuck. I'm sorry, Zara. Okay? I'm sorry for not respecting your boundaries and for suffocating you."

I say nothing, waiting for him to continue down the long list of things he should apologize for. This is the first major fight we've ever gotten in, but a simple sorry isn't going to change anything. The only thing that's going to fix this is for him to actually listen to what I've been trying to say and for him to respect my boundaries and my life.

I've said it until I'm blue in the face, and I'm not wasting my breath on another conversation when he doesn't seem really interested in changing his behavior.

Oliver drags a hand down his face exasperatedly, heaving a sigh. He honestly looks... ragged. "I'm really sorry. It's just you're my baby sister, Zar. I know you're only one year younger than me, but I feel like I need to look out for you and make sure you don't find yourself in any bullshit. I know I'm overprotective, I really do, but it's just because I worry about you."

Rookie Mistake

I only start to feel slightly bad when I see the sincerity on his face, but it's still not enough to overshadow the shitshow from the last few months.

I'm just empathetic, and I hate this ridiculous rift between us. I'm angry and frustrated, but more than anything, I'm hurt that he so blatantly disregarded my feelings and boundaries.

"Look, I appreciate that, Oliver, I do, but this has to stop, okay? Whatever issue you have with Davis, please let it go. It's not just hurting you, but it's hurting him too. And all of this? It's hurting *me*. I really don't want to permanently move to the dorms with Harp, but I will, Oliver. I really will if that's what it takes to make you back off. Please just trust me to make my own decisions. You act like I'm an out-of-control idiot who can't be trusted. Just because I'm younger doesn't mean I'm less capable of making good choices."

He doesn't immediately respond, just stares out past me to something behind me before he finally drags his gaze back to mine. "Okay. I understand, and I promise, I'll stop. I really mean it, Zara. I hear you. But can you just stop hiding shit from me? I felt blindsided by it last night."

"Then stop making me *have* to hide things."

"Okay. I won't. But Zar, just because you're into him, it doesn't mean that I'm going to apologize and become best friends with the guy."

I shrug. "Fine. I didn't ask you to be. I'm just asking

that you let me live my life and that you respect any and all boundaries that I lay down. You're not responsible for my actions, Oliver, and you can't control me by forcing me into something that I don't want. Davis and I are officially a couple now, and if you still want to be a part of my life, then you'll be civil and stop putting me in the middle of something that has *nothing* to do with me."

Oliver doesn't look happy about the fact that Davis and I are officially dating, but guess what?

It's not his decision, and he gets no opinion on what I do with my love life.

Ever. Again.

"Just give me a little time to come around to it, Zar. I promise I'll back off and respect your boundaries and choices." He pauses, unshed tears shining in his green eyes. "You're my baby sister, and you're my best friend, and I know I've been a real asshole the last few months, but I just feel like you're slipping away from me and growing up and leaving me behind."

My shoulders fall when I sigh, blowing out a pent-up breath and shaking my head. Oliver's been an asshole, and my trust in him isn't what it once was, but he's still my brother.

He's still my best friend. Even if I want to throttle him. He's still the guy who spent most of his middle school years with his nails painted because he let me practice on him. He's the guy who learned how to braid my hair so he could do it himself because I would cry when we brushed out the tangles.

"I love you, Ollie," I say as I throw my arms around his neck and hold him tightly to me. "And I'm not going anywhere. Life is just... changing. I'm growing and evolving, but one thing that never will change is that you'll *always* be my big brother. I just need you to respect me... That's it, okay?"

His arms slide around my waist at some point, hugging me back, and we stay like that for a few beats, neither of us wanting to end the moment. I feel lighter after the last few months of tension and frustration being the only conversations we've shared.

"So we're good?" he asks when he pulls back and quickly swipes at a tear that's fallen onto his cheek. He'd never actually admit that he just cried over our relationship, but he soooo did.

And now, I'm never going to let him live it down.

What are little sisters for if it isn't driving their older brother nuts?

"Not to kick you out, and I'm so glad that you came here and we talked everything over, but Davis is supposed to be here any minute, and I'd like to avoid any awkwardness."

Oliver nods begrudgingly. "I understand. If you need me, no matter what, I'll be here, Zar. Night or day. I'll come get you from a bar, from a frat party. Don't ever forget that. Will you please think about moving back home?"

"Okay, I will, I promise. Love you, Ollie," I whisper as I put my head on his chest once again, wrapping my arms around his surly shoulders.

"Love you too, Zar."

A few minutes later, he's gone, leaving me staring out at the empty hallway, partially in shock and feeling a sliver of *relief*. As prideful as Oliver is, I didn't expect him to be the one to apologize, so I'm really surprised that he did.

I'm glad that we attempted to patch things up between us, but the true test will be if Oliver actually changes these things, not just says them.

Words are nothing without actions.

After I close the door, I walk back into Harper's dorm, which is more like a closet with a bed. There are clothes littering nearly every surface, and yet when I scoured through them in search of something to wear for my first official date with Davis tonight, I found absolutely nothing.

Everything's too pink and girly, definitely not my style, but I did find a vintage-looking band T-shirt shoved in the very back of her dresser, so I went with it.

And actually... it looks *so* fucking fire.

It's long enough to fall to my thighs, so I paired it with some fishnets and the only pair of shoes I grabbed before coming to stay here, my old checkered Vans that have music notes I doodled on the soles with a permanent marker.

I even curled my hair and put on Davis's favorite shade of lipstick. The combination of all of that has me feeling confident and not at all nervous.

Sure, it's our first *"official"* date, but we've been secretly seeing each other for several weeks now, and let's be honest, we've done more stuff together than some couples do in a lifetime, so I'm comfortable around him.

A few minutes later, there's a light knock at the door, and when I open it and see him standing on the other side, a flurry of butterflies erupts in my stomach.

It'll never get old. That feeling. It always feels like the first night we met.

"Hi," he murmurs as his eyes drag down my body. "Damn, baby, you look hot as fuck. Big night?"

Smirking, I do a little spin, showing off the outfit with a shrug. "Oh, you know, just going on a date with this guy."

He smirks, pulling his hand from his jeans pockets and reaching for me. His big palm splays along my waist and hauls me forward into his hard, muscled front.

That will also never get old.

My boyfriend is actually the hottest man alive. No question.

"Might wanna tell him I can fight, then, Trouble." His breath fans against my lips.

I rise on my toes and murmur against his mouth, "Mmmm. We'll see how the night goes first."

"Brat."

He captures my lips as his arm tightens around my waist, holding me close to him. I swear I can feel his heart racing alongside mine. When his hand slides to my ass and the kiss starts to turn heated, he stops, pulling back abruptly.

"Fuck, we need to go before we never leave this dorm. Something tells me that Harper wouldn't want me fucking you on every surface of her room."

"Yeah, probably not. There's always later though." I wink. I turn back inside, grabbing my small purse from the top of the desk, and turn back toward him. "Well, let's go, Loverboy. I've got a date to get to."

True to his word, Davis takes me to Magnolia's for our first official date. It's the perfect choice, and I've convinced myself that he might be perfect too.

Like the last time he brought me here, we're sitting on the hood of his truck in the parking lot, listening to an old playlist. Only this time… he's mine.

And I'm his.

"Oh my god, this is my favorite song. Dance with me?" I ask, jumping up from the hood and holding my hand out toward him. "Nothing's Going to Hurt You

Baby" plays through the speakers as he slides his hand in mine.

He pulls me against him and laces our fingers together before lifting my hand to his mouth and pressing a kiss to the back of it.

It's so sweet I nearly melt at his feet in a puddle.

We sway to the slow, sensual beat, our eyes locked. One of my favorite songs has new meaning, and I love it.

"Feels kind of full circle, doesn't it?"

I nod. "It does. Who knew that bidding on you in an auction would lead to… this."

"That *was* a shit ton of money," he teases.

"Yeah." I shrug. "I think it was worth it though. It got us here, didn't it?"

Lowering his lips to mine, he says, "Yeah, Trouble. It did. And I'm *so* fucking glad you're mine."

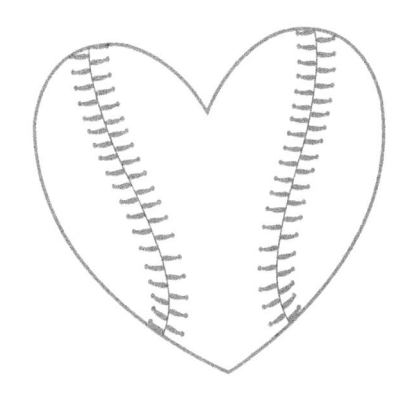

epilogue
Davis

6 months later

There are few things that feel the way it does to stand in the middle of a stadium packed with ten thousand people, all chanting your name as you strike out the third guy in a row.

In fact, I think the only thing that feels better than that is when Zara's lips are wrapped around my cock, and that's only because there's nothing else in the world like my girlfriend.

Fuck, I *love* her.

And I love playing for the best team in the NCAA.

I love being a Hellcat, and this season has been fucking incredible. A constant high that I never want to come down from.

"Hey, Loverboy," Zara squeals as she jumps into my arms, locking her legs around my waist. "God, you were so hot out there. I couldn't wait another second to pounce on you."

I chuckle, reaching up to brush her hair out of her face. "Yeah? I was just showing off because I knew you were watching."

That's actually true. I always play better when I know my girl's watching, and maybe that's why I've had the best season of my career. Because Zara hasn't missed a single game.

She's been in the stands, cheering me on, being my biggest fan.

Love does funny things to a person. Honestly, I can hardly remember the kind of guy I was before I met her. Before she stomped into my life in those fucking combat boots and I served her my heart on a plate from Magnolia's.

I never stood a chance.

It's been hers ever since, and the past six months have been the happiest months of my life.

She's made me the happiest I've ever been.

"You look so sexy wearing this," I say, dragging my fingers down the front of her open jersey, over my number that's scrawled along the chest. "I love seeing you wear my jersey."

Her lip curves into a grin, and I lean in, capturing

her lips because I can't wait another fucking second to kiss her.

"Good," she murmurs against my lips when she pulls away, trailing hot, wet kisses along my jawline until she gets to my ear. "I was thinking I could wear it while you fuck my tits and come on my face later."

Motherfucker.

I groan. "You are fucking trouble."

"Always have been and always will be. Good thing you love trouble, huh?" she muses, a playful smirk on her lips as she lowers herself to her feet, brushing over my hardening dick.

This girl. She's going to kill me one day.

"Yeah, I do. But not when we're about to go to dinner with your parents and brother. Now we're actually able to sit in the same room without wanting to throat punch each other," I say, reaching for my bat bag near my feet, then hoisting it on my shoulder and grabbing her hand.

I love the way she feels in my hands. Like she was made to be mine.

Perfect.

"Thank you," she murmurs. "For making an effort to get along with him. It means a lot to me."

We're walking to my truck now, hand in hand, and my shoulder dips. "He's not… as bad as I once thought he was. But don't tell him that, or he'll think we're, I don't know, friends or something."

She doesn't respond, simply smirks as she lifts a brow.

Fine, we're kind of, *sort of* friends.

Turns out we have way more things in common than hating each other, and since I'm dating his sister and we're teammates, we're around each other more than not.

We play video games sometimes and... *occasionally* send funny memes to each other in secret.

It's better this way though. I didn't want Zara to feel uncomfortable or like she had to choose between us, and if I have any say-so in it, she's going to be mine forever.

I don't care that it's only been six months.

When I think of my future?

It's Zara.

Of all the uncertainties the future holds, I know that part for a fact.

She makes me better.

We leave the stadium in a hurry since there's not much time between my game and dinner with her parents and head to my house. Most of the guys haven't made it home yet, so we're alone.

Which is rare and hard to come by these days. Even more of a reason for me to convince her to get an apartment with me next year.

"Let's go shower," she says as we walk into my

Rookie Mistake

bedroom. I pause, tossing my bag onto the floor near my closet, and shoot her a look.

As if we have time for me to blow her back out before dinner.

There's no such thing as a quickie with us. There are multiple orgasms and lots of foreplay involved.

"Not being late for dinner with your parents, baby."

She rakes her teeth over her bottom lip and reaches beneath her jersey, unclasping her bra and dropping it to the floor.

Fuck.

"It'll be a bad impression. I want them to like me," I say, swallowing roughly. I'm fucked. I know it, she knows it. I couldn't tell her no if there was a gun to my head.

Next, the button on her jean shorts is flicked open, and she's dragging them down her hips until they pool at her feet. Stepping out of them, she saunters over to me.

"Guess I'll have to make myself come, then."

Motherfucker.

I reach for the back of my T-shirt and pull it over my head, shedding the rest of my clothes in five seconds flat as she does the same.

We might just make a quickie happen today with how pressed for time we are.

"What is this?" she asks, running her fingers over the small white bandage along my hip. Her gaze lifts to mine, and that cute-as-fuck space between her brows furrows.

I just smile, dipping my shoulder.

"Did you get hurt and I missed it? What happ—"

"Take it off," I interrupt her. "See for yourself."

Her gaze holds mine for a beat more before she gently pulls off the gauze, realization morphing her face. "Is that…"

Her eyes dart to mine. Piercing green, the most beautiful color I've ever seen. "It is."

"Davis… you got my *music* tattooed on you?"

I nod as I reach for her, grasping her chin between my fingers. "Music's the most important part of you, Zara, and… *you're* the most important part of me. I love you."

Tears coat her cheeks, and she shakes her head, laughing in disbelief. "I love you so much. I… I can't believe you did this. It's beautiful."

"I knew that I was in trouble the moment that I laid eyes on you, Zara Andrews. And I've never loved Trouble more."

Binge the **completed** Orleans University series today by clicking here!

Want a sneak peek into Chapter 1 of Homerun Proposal? Flip the page!

homerun proposal
Hallie

"I'm pretty sure it's *staring* at me," Vivienne mutters, peeking through one squinted eye. "How is it possible that a..." She leans in and whispers like we're in a crowd of people and not alone in my room. "*Penis*... is looking at me like I owe it something."

I cringe when she uses the word "penis." I'm pretty sure, aside from the word "moist," that penis is the ugliest word in the entire English language.

"This was *your* idea," I remind her, not dragging my eyes away from the screen of my laptop, which currently has a man thrusting into a woman from behind as she moans obnoxiously loud. The sounds of their mingled breathing and skin slapping fill my room. Surely, *this* can't be what everyone raves about, right?

Sex.

Intercourse.

Lovemaking.

Something I know nothing about beyond the basic mechanics that I've learned in sex ed and movies and from the birds-and-the-bees talk with my parents, which I'm *still* scarred from.

I, Hallie Jo Edwards, am still *very* much a virgin, even though I'm a freshman at Orleans University. Isn't college where everyone loses their virginity?

Eighteen years old and never been kissed.

How is that even possible?

Well, very easily, if you're *me*.

Me... the girl who chooses to stay home from a party just to finish a spooky cross-stitch and the kind of girl who has no less than thirty tabs of Dramione fanfic open at once. The girl who considers black and purple the only primary colors on the color wheel. The very same girl who survives on conspiracies, Sour Punch straws, and nineties alternative on an iPod shuffle. Talk about outdated.

Not exactly dickbait.

But I'm good with it. I'm totally comfortable floating to my own tune at the beat of my own drum.

I mean, I'm awesome.

And by awesome, I mean the never-been-kissed, college-freshman-virgin kind of way.

"I've seen lots of them, but this thing looks like an untamed dragon. Someone get this man a leash for this *beast*," Viv says as a shudder racks her body.

I shrug. "It is kind of... *wild*."

We both look at each other, then die.

Absolutely lose our shit, giggles escaping until we're both in a heap on my bed with tears streaming down our faces.

Out of all of the ideas that my best friend has ever had, this by far is the weirdest. It's one thing to watch porn on your own, but it's an entirely different ball game when you're doing it with your best friend who has the maturity level of a fourteen-year-old boy.

"Hal?" a deep voice calls from the other side of my door, and then it swings open, and Eli, my other best friend, strides through without waiting for a response.

I reach for my computer so quickly that I accidentally push Viv off the side of the bed in desperation to slam the screen shut before Eli realizes what we were doing. In my haste, I slam my finger inside my computer and squeal.

"Shit. Fuck. *Damnit.*" I suck the tip into my mouth to dull the ache as I jump from my bed and push the computer all the way off the other side.

It lands on the floor with a thump.

Eli looks from me to Vivienne on the floor in front of him, who is desperately trying to hold it together, to the discarded laptop, then back at me, his brow furrowed in confusion. "Uhh... What's going on? What are you watching, and why did you just freak out when I walked in?"

Silence greets his question until Viv loses it. She's the

first one to go, her laugh exploding out of her like a poorly timed bomb. She shakes her head as she pants between breaths, "We're watching porn. *Terrible* porn at that."

Her words are merely a string of wheezes somehow formed together into a sentence, and I groan as I watch a devilish smirk slide onto Eli's face.

Great. Now this is a *group* porn-watching session. I settle back onto the bed and wish momentarily that it would swallow me up so I could avoid the mortification I'm currently experiencing.

Without another word, he waltzes through the door, then slams it shut with his foot and steps over Viv, making a beeline straight for the bed.

He rubs his hands together in anticipation as he dives in next to me, putting his arms behind his head. "So, what we watching? A little girl-on-girl action? Maybe a little double penetration?"

My eyes widen as I stutter, "*D-double?*"

"Don't freak her out, Eli. Jesus," Viv mutters as she walks over to the side of the bed my laptop fell to, picking it up and reopening it. The screen resumes the poorly filmed and recorded amateur sex tape we're watching.

"Wow." Eli blows out a breath, squinting at the screen. "That guy's got some serious fucking stamina."

"Yeah, I mean, look at the muscles in his ass. You could crack an egg on those babies." Viv nudges Eli to scoot over, and she slides in beside him, crossing her legs. "If only this was actually how it went."

His chest rumbles with a scoff. "Just because *you've* had bad sex doesn't mean it's like that for everyone else, Vivienne."

That's right. I'm the only virgin left of my best friends, and I am painfully aware of the fact.

Viv sticks her tongue out at him and flips him the finger.

"At least you've had *bad* sex. I've had *no* sex, which is even worse," I mutter to the both of them.

Eli's gaze turns to me. "It's not a big deal, Hal. Tons of people wait for the right person."

I love him, I do. And I appreciate him saying that, but he just… doesn't get it.

Sighing heavily, I say, "I'm just over it. Being the tagalong, the sweet, 'aw, she's cute,' alas awkward and pathetically alone Hallie Jo."

Viv tilts her head. "Which is why I've got the *perfect* plan." She rises from the bed and spins to face me. "Hal, we're in college. We're freshmen at one of the best universities in the South. Together. We need to get out and *live*. Go to parties, drink way too much cheap liquor. *Kiss* hot boys. Get pointless tattoos that we never regret when we're old and wrinkly, despite what the boomers think. Be young while we have the opportunity. You know, before real life starts."

In theory, it sounds great. Easy even.

Like, technically speaking, how hard could it be to find a party on a college campus, cheap liquor in a red Solo cup, and a hot guy who's more than willing to stick his tongue down your throat?

That's not the hard part.

You see, it's got everything to do with me.

I'm just kind of… me. And I already know that I'm not everyone's cup of tea.

Honestly, I'm probably more like kombucha if I had to categorize myself.

Bitter at first taste but then slowly starts to grow on you after you hold your nose and force it down.

I mean, it is fermented bacteria that's good for you. Gross, but not bad after a while.

But Viv is right.

This is supposed to be the prime time in our lives. The time to sow our wild oats, to let our hair down and live it up before the societally imposed walls of adulthood close in on us.

"She's right, Hal. At least about living it up while you can. Get out, see what the world has to offer you. I'll come, too, and look out for you two. Make sure you're having fun. Safely," Eli adds.

I chew on the corner of my lip as I mull over what they're saying.

I know that they're both right… It just seems much easier to talk about than it actually is to do it. Putting yourself out there, forgetting the things that hold you back. Pretending you're not scared that the world will reject you for being yourself.

Finally, I drag my gaze up, flickering between the two of them. "You're right. Both of you. Let's do it." I exhale, letting the nerves go. "Tomorrow, we're going to go to a party."

Her eyes light up like I just told her we're about to meet Ed and Lorraine Warren back from the dead. "Really?"

I nod.

"We're going to a *frat* party, and we're not leaving until you're no longer an eighteen-year-old college freshman who's never been kissed. Welcome to the first day of the rest of your life, Hallie Jo Edwards."

"This sounds oddly reassuring yet ominous at once," I say at the same time *"Pizza's here!"* is yelled from the foyer, signaling our highly anticipated dinner is finally here. Together, we all get up from my bed, abandoning the laptop. "Now, can we *please* go stuff our faces with pizza? I'm starving, and I want to do more research for this week's episode."

Eli laughs, tucking his arm around my neck and dragging me against his side as we follow behind Viv to the kitchen. Sometimes I forget how much I need an Eli hug. It always makes me feel better, and admitting all of that out loud was hard, even if I don't want to show it. Growth is rarely ever easy.

Viv heads straight for the fridge and pulls out an orange Fanta, one of our many obsessions.

"I've been listening to a nonfiction book this week and taking a few notes in preparation. I think this episode will have more listeners than ever before, judging by the amount of hype it's getting on social media. Also, I've got to head out after this. Another calculus tutoring session, and go figure, the guy giving it is a complete perv," she says as she sits at the table and throws open the pizza box, reaching in for a large slice, then pushing one my way.

I grab my slice and take a giant bite, closing my eyes and moaning around the mouthful of extra cheesy, greasy goodness.

"Bigfoot this week, right?" Lane Collins's voice booms behind me, announcing his presence, scaring the absolute shit out of me to where I begin to choke on the mouthful of pizza.

I'm hacking, and Viv's eyes widen as I try desperately to get the food unlodged to no avail.

Holy shit, I'm going to die literally choking on cheesy pizza with black olives.

I'm going to die a *virgin*.

"Shit, are you okay, Hal?" Eli rushes over, tossing his still-empty plate onto the table and pulling me from my chair. His arms circle my waist as he begins to perform the Heimlich.

The piece of pizza that seemed much smaller when I

was only chewing it and not choking finally becomes unlodged from my throat and flies out onto the ground with a disgusting squelch.

Air invades my lungs, and I sink back into Eli's arms as relief floods me.

I'm okay. I'm safe. I'm with Eli. It's okay.

I'm still trying to catch my breath when I look over at Lane, leaning against the counter, promptly sucking out all of the air that I've just managed to inhale after my near-death experience.

He has that effect about him, walking into a room and stealing everyone's attention and the ability to breathe.

Maybe he just has that effect on *me*, but judging by the number of girls that sneak out of our off-campus house in the middle of the night, it's *not* just me.

You see, for as long as I can remember, I've been harboring a small... innocent little crush on my best friend's older brother, and it's a secret that I'll likely take to my grave.

Because Lane Collins would *never* look my way.

I've only ever been his little brother's best friend, the one who's tagged along since we were kids. The annoying neighbor girl that he could never seem to get rid of, not even as he got older and his parents forced him to let Eli and me tag along to the movies, to the mall, to the field when he played.

I *cherished* those moments because even for just a few

minutes, I was in his orbit. I existed right along with the girls that threw themselves at his feet. I would be the recipient of the dimpled smile he reserved for those girls, and I would hold on to those moments like it was a lifeline, simply tiding me over until the next second of attention I could steal from him.

"What's up, Hal?" He smirks, those damned dimples popping as he reaches into the cabinet and pulls out his favorite shaker bottle. I try not to notice that he's shirtless, and his wide chest is on display for my eyes to devour.

Try being the operative word.

It's impossible not to notice how perfectly defined his chest is and how the muscles in his arms flex and ripple every time he moves.

"She almost just choked to death on a piece of pizza," Eli says, shaking his head as he rubs my back. Clearly, he's well acquainted with the fact that my clumsy awkwardness truly knows no bounds.

Lane raises his all-too-perfect eyebrow. "So, just another Thursday, then?"

"Yep."

Assholes.

This is what I get for living with these two. Well, not that I really had much choice. Since I wasn't in any rush to live with a stranger in a tiny dorm on campus, my parents and the Collinses decided that the best place for me to live was right here with Eli and Lane, who already had an off-campus house. I wouldn't have to room with someone I didn't know, and they could look after me since this is the first time I've lived outside of my parents' house.

A situation that worked great for everyone.

Theoretically.

I spend most of my days trying *not* to fantasize about Lane and the rest of the time trying to focus on the ridiculous freshman course load I've taken on as a film production student. I got waitlisted at my dream school, NYU, so I opted for my second choice, and I'm hoping to get my prereqs out the way so I get accepted as a second-year transfer. Which means that I have to work extra hard to make sure my portfolio is ready and my GPA is high.

Reaching for the kitchen chair, I pull it out and flop down into it, blowing my bangs out of my face while doing so. My eyes drift to Lane at the stove, working on his protein shake, his gray sweatpants slung haphazardly low on his waist, revealing the Adonis belt of his hips.

Something tells me that he would look nothing like the man from today's *porn debacle*. That he would be the kind of guy who'd talk filthy to you while he did despicable things to your body. My face begins to flame as I imagine the two of us in that video, doing the things that the couple on the screen did.

The feel of his hands gripping my hips as he thrust into me, his eyes devouring me an—

"So, we still on for our Friday movie night, Hal?" Eli mumbles through a mouthful of pizza, mentioning our decade-long weekend tradition that jolts me from my dirty images of his brother.

Jesus Christ. My heart drops to my stomach as if everyone in the room can read my thoughts.

In the short time that I've been here, it's been a rare occasion for us to all be together for a meal since all of us have vastly different schedules. Especially since it's preseason and Lane is Orleans University's star pitcher.

When he's not working out, practicing, or in study hall, he's with his friends at a party or with his flavor of the night.

"Yep. Viv and I finished discussing things for this week's episode, so I should be good." I open the orange Fanta she slid to me and take another much smaller bite of the greasy pizza.

Some college kids love ramen, and then there's me. I'm surviving on strong will and Jack's Pizza.

Eli shoves another bite into his mouth, chewing quickly before speaking. "Cool. I heard there's this new documentary called *Fantastic Fungi* that I think you'd like."

That *he* would like, and that will undoubtedly make me pass out within thirty minutes of the moment he presses Play, but whatever.

Honestly, who in their right mind would choose to watch a documentary on fungus growing out of the ground for *fun* on a Friday night?

Eli Collins. That's who.

"Can't wait," I say despite my true feelings, plastering on a wide smile. At the end of the day, I love to spend time with Eli. He's my best friend and has been since we were just toddlers, and if he wants to bore me to death during our weekly movie night, fine.

"What are you up to this weekend, bro?" Eli asks his brother, who's still standing at the counter.

Lane's tanned shoulder dips. "Coach wants me icing my shoulder, so I'll probably come back early and get some sleep. Who knows, might hit a party up. Find a cleat chaser to sneak out." He shoots me a pointed gaze, his lips tugging up in a grin.

And there you have it, ladies and gentlemen. America's *sweetheart*.

This is the guy that every single female at Orleans University would trip over their feet to have a chance with.

He's charismatic, even when he's being a douchebag, and that is a special skill that only guys like Lane possess.

"Shouldn't you be studying or, I dunno, doing something *productive*?" Viv asks.

A smug smirk sits on his lips as he taps his finger

along his temple. "I don't have to study, Viv, not when I've got a brain like this."

"Runs in the family," Eli adds cockily.

Truly, how is Lane so smart *and* so attractive? It's not fair to us normal, average humans who actually have to apply effort in order to get a passing grade.

The Collins brothers share the same unruly dirty-blond hair and almost the same shade of brilliant emerald eyes. Both have strong jaws and tanned skin that is from genetics and not the sun. But that's where the similarities end. They couldn't be any more different if they tried.

Eli is more reserved and nerdy, while his brother is outgoing, cocky, and the life of the party. Both are handsome and smart, even if Lane likes to pretend he's just a dumb jock for the sake of his campus reputation.

I know better only because I grew up next door, and I see the side of Lane that he chooses not to share with the world. As Eli's best friend, I've spent as much time in their house as I have my own. I'm lost in thought, popping the bracelets on my wrist, when Lane turns toward me.

"Nice bracelets, Hallie Jo," he muses, then downs the glass of water in one gulp, the strong column of his throat bobbing as he swallows.

My cheeks immediately heat. He's being sarcastic and teasing me because of the beaded bracelets on my wrist that Viv and I make when we're binge-watching

Netflix. Maybe it's childish, but we have fun doing it and seeing who can put the most absurd shit on them.

One guess who's currently winning that bet. The unhinged one. Aka *Vivienne*.

"Uh, thanks?" I say quietly, my eyes flitting to Viv, who's squinting at him. "They're just, uh... a silly thing we do for fun."

"They're cute." His smirk widens into a full-blown smile, and once again, it feels hard to breathe.

Cute. Lane Collins just said something on my body is *cute*.

Before I can even really begin to obsess over his comment, Viv pastes on a mischievous smile. "Are you going to the Kappa party this weekend? Me, Hallie, and Eli are going."

"You two are going to a *frat* party?" he says, disbelief lacing his tone while his eyebrows nearly meet his hairline.

I roll my eyes. "Don't look so surprised. We're allowed to have a social life too, Lane."

Holding his hands up in surrender, he shakes his head. "Just wondering. Not really your scene, huh?"

I shrug as I drop my gaze. "I'm just... trying out some new things."

"Like hooking up with hot boys." Viv giggles as she wiggles her eyebrows suggestively. She stands from her chair and walks to the trash to throw away the plate.

"Gotta run, or I'm going to be late for my tutoring session. Send me all the good vibes, please."

We all say goodbye, and I escape to my bedroom, where I shut the door behind me and head straight for the window. I climb out carefully, placing my foot onto the awning and then onto the flat slope of the roof.

Since starting at Orleans University, this spot has become my favorite place in the world to be. High enough that I can see the entire campus, and at night, the stars shine bright in a blanket above me.

I don't know how long I sit out here, my knees pressed against my chest, watching the sun fade into the clouds as dusk appears.

Long enough to where my butt has gone numb and I've twisted the little pink alien pendant around my neck into knots. A nervous habit.

A sound behind me pulls me from my thoughts, and I turn back to see Eli climbing through the window, and then he's joining me on the asphalt shingles, resting his forearms on his legs as he peers out at the glittering lights of campus.

Neither of us speaks for a minute, the sound of cars passing on the highway drowning out my thoughts. It's a comfortable silence, and that's part of what I love about my friendship with Eli. It just feels... natural. It's always been like this between us. *Easy.*

"Hal?"

I glance over at him, his piercing green eyes seeing

right into my soul. Or at least that's what it feels like sometimes.

He bumps my shoulder with his. "You feeling weird after that conversation?"

Shrugging, I finger the bracelets on my wrist but say nothing.

"Viv was only joking, Hal. You know how she is. You don't *actually* have to hook up with anyone. Being a virgin isn't a big deal, you know? This is your life and something that's important to you. Things should happen when *you* feel ready, not because you feel like you need to prove something or to be anyone other than who you are."

"I know. I just feel… like, am I still a virgin because I'm weird? Am I really just that awkward?"

"Hallie." He blanches. "Fuck no. You're one of the most incredible people I know. You're smart and funny and beautiful. I mean… the whole package."

Tossing me a playful smirk, he reaches out and threads his hand in mine. Not in a romantic way, but in a comforting way. A way that has always just been… us. Something he learned early on, that physical touch is my love language.

"I'm just tired of blending into the wall like a glorified wallflower. I'm just *tired*, Eli. I want to experience all the things that I never have, and I feel this… I don't know, push inside me for more. Not just my…" I lower my voice, clearing my throat in hesitation. "*Virginity*. I mean just in life. I want to be more than a wallflower. I want to spread my wings and fly. Grow into the person I'm meant to be. Find out who I really am. You know, all the important things."

Eli's fingers tighten in mine, and he nods. "I know, and I support anything you decide, Hallie. I always have, and I always will. Just be true to yourself. That's all I'm saying."

"I know. And I don't think I could take on college without you by my side," I tell him.

"Anyone who is lucky enough to be a part of your universe will know exactly what they have from the moment you walk in."

And just like that, it hits me why it is that Eli Collins has always been the rock in my life.

Because he makes me feel like I'm the best version of myself.

Want to keep reading and find out what sweet, quirky Hallie gets herself into?

Homerun Proposal is FREE on KU. Click here to read!

need moore?

Want instant access to bonus scenes, exclusive giveaways, and content you can't find ANYWHERE else?

Sign up for my newsletter here and get all of the goods!

In your audiobook era? Find all of my audiobooks here!

Want to chat with me about life, get exclusive giveaways and see behind the scenes content? Join my reader group Give Me Moore

also by maren moore

Totally Pucked

Change on the Fly

Sincerely, The Puck Bunny

The Scorecard

The Final Score

The Penalty Shot

Playboy Playmaker

Orleans U

Homerun Proposal

Catching Feelings

Walkoff Wedding

Standalone

The Enemy Trap

The Newspaper Nanny

Strawberry Hollow

The Mistletoe Bet

A Festive Feud

The Christmas List

about the author

Maren Moore is an Amazon Top 20 Best-selling sports romance author. Her books are packed full of heat and all the feels that will always come with a happily ever after. She resides in southern Louisiana with her husband, two little boys and their fur babies. When she isn't on a deadline, she's probably reading yet another Dramione fan fic, rewatching cult classic horror movies, or daydreaming about the 90's.

You can connect with her on social media or find information on her books here ➡ here.

Printed in Great Britain
by Amazon